the
young
fate

the young fate

scott b robinson

ISBN: 979-8-218-18672-2 (Paperback)
ISBN: 979-8-218-18671-5 (eBook)

Any references to historical events, real people, or real places are used fictitiously. Names, characters, and places are products of the author's imagination.

Book design by Scott B. Robinson.

Printed by Ruy Lopez Editions, in the United States of America.

First printing edition 2023.
fireandart.net

for my sons

Qui pleur là, sinon le vent simple, à cette heure
Seule, avec diamants extrêmes?...Mais qui pleur,
Si proche de moi-même au moment de pleurer?

—*La Jeune Parque*, Paul Valéry

When my brother died, I became my
brother. I did what he wished to do.

—King Bhumibol Adulyadej

the young fate

One

Yan's mother told him she owned but two true things in life: him, her only son, and debt. Yan found it a strange counting of one's blessings, though it wasn't any conspicuous omission that gave him pause. It was the growing debt rather that left him anxious deep inside. Once the rent and groceries and bills had all been paid, his mother appeared unwilling to resist squandering any meager remnant, and then some, on some little self-indulgence. Nor could Yan begrudge her. She worked harder than about anyone he knew. But the boy did nonetheless surmise how, at the rate his mom was going, she'd end up caught off-guard by life's inevitable misfortunes and their inevitably large expenses. The son prayed her spiritual funds might outlive her fiscal.

Who else would she have had if not for him? Her two jobs had strained the few superficial friendships she'd abandoned along with more carefree years. No relatives were left in the city either, except her one last sister, whom she hadn't spoken to in ages. As for everyone else, as for all those strangers she crossed paths with or served day in and out, each in turn polite but indifferent—what joy did they afford when they were the very thing tearing her from the one face (tiny round, soft-eyed) she yearned to fondle? Long ago she'd sipped its bitterness: the more she resolved to provide, the farther apart they had to grow. Her presence in her son's life was next to nonexistent anymore, which she presumed must make him equally sorrowful.

Some evenings still, when her son might fall asleep with his head on her lap, it was easier for the woman to wallow in this restorative misconception than to speculate Yan might not feel entirely the same. Don't let this be the last, she incanted internally, almost intoxicated with the moment. If only she could peer inside, then she might see what all this sentiment was worth. Then might she understand the extent of her absence, at least as manifested in Yan's dreams, which were simply a mirror to his waking days. Because in the end, the mother's neglect had opened up vast swaths of time to the boy, free from the prying eyes of any grownup, when for long spells she had no idea where her wandering son was. Nor what he was up to.

There had been an age when the notion would have terrified the child.

*

Yan had spent most that afternoon wandering all the way up from Petchburi. He now sat on the sidewalk's margins, drawing in his pad of paper beneath the shadow of the train station stairwell, studying the motorbikes as they flowed clockwise through the roundabout encircling Victory Monument. He depicted with an erratic stroke how they streamed between stalled cars and buses. From every corner of his eye, the vast metropolis burgeoning, one partially erected skyscraper after another pulling itself up to the heavens. The spectacle and din were absolute. But if the child turned his eyes away and down to the page upon his lap, however unequal he might judge his own creation, the whole instead was peaceful, silent, still.

Above, a lean wisp of cloud tore the burning blue of the endless sky.

And it was precisely then when, out from the monstrous world that mocks all musing and demands one's undivided attention, a black-and-white cat meandered her way from behind the street stalls, up to the curb where the child was. He could tell the stray was female because her belly hung plump, expectant with a litter from an otherwise scrawny frame. She showed an unusual trust, seeking shelter from the clamor, perhaps because she craved a little affection. Yan set his pen and pad aside, grasped her beneath the forelegs and pulled her onto his lap tenderly. The two sat there together on the rim unseen. At times he dangled the amulet strung around his neck before her playful paws. Or sometimes they watched and listened to the traffic spin untiringly around the giant stone obelisk.

It all seemed like a pointless race through time. An obsession with the mania of life, all perfectly hurried and haphazard, yet complacent and divorced from it all. Profound nonchalance. Who can say when it first sprung forth? This human momentum that's flowed from generation to generation, this psychological rhythm that's floated downriver since before Lord Buddha was born. Now it pulses in Bangkok's million trees. Now their sovereign canopy chants it in unison with the senseless breeze off the commotion below…*life after life after life after life*…Yan couldn't fathom how he might ever hope to trace that myriad of leaves.

Reincarnation or no, one is only allotted so much time in this particular life, in this here world. The more you pretend to ignore it, the more your dwindling hours tighten around your heart like an invisible serpent. For what else all of lifetime's tireless bows and appeasing smiles? Just to ward against whatever bit of karma that might lay waiting coiled in the grass?

We are taught that aspects of life are like a dream. You could see it in the passing faces, in their eyes. Their brains were crammed so full of fantasies, of countless, infinitely tiny fantasies: mundane fantasies, secret fantasies; fantasies long dwelled upon, fleeting subconscious ones; fantasies of the past, of things to come. There is not space within the span of a lifetime to realize them all. And no matter what the heavens permit to materialize on earth, up till the last breath, all those impenetrable glances crave to behold a little more. Just a little more of this finite life, the crumbling hole from which they're forever climbing, daylight's close always nearing.

Aren't some of these ideas the kind one hardly noticeable boy and cat might meditate upon together, to the extent of each their faculties at least? Perhaps these notions surfaced as mere inklings, shadows of less formally pursued speculations.

A loud train screeched down the concrete railway overhead and the animal leapt from Yan's lap. When he looked up, he caught sight of a feather floating midway in the air—from some unseen flown bird. When had it appeared? So delicate and inconsequential was the grey blur of a thing, no other soul could have noticed. It hovered within a distinct space just above the traffic, never rising nor sinking much. How long could it levitate? Yan imagined that if he stayed focused on it, it might remain, long into the night, never to fall to the street to be crushed beneath some random rolling tire. He felt he ought to uncap his pen and capture it on paper fast.

But then he began to imagine that only if he turned away instead, forgot about that scrap torn from a wing, then alone might it sustain its magic flight.

Chapter 2: Friend in Need

An imperfect ring of five boys snickered amongst themselves intermittently, like a frisky swarm of mosquitoes, while dodging a barrage of assaults from the kid in the middle swinging a broomstick broadly. A red kerchief was tied about the latter's eyes—they were playing blind man's bluff. And the closer the gang lured the blindfolded Toi to the brink of the sidewalk, the harder he dashed his stick toward the taunting shapeless voices. He had to aim high if he was going to catch one of them on the ear or in the nose. Toi was small for his age.

When Yan first saw Toi thus from a distance, smack in the middle of another predicament, he knew Toi was taking his adversaries' bait, looming perilously over an abrupt break in the concrete. Yan suspected his friend might have some last trick up his sleeve but couldn't muster the confidence to wait out that hunch. He brushed where the amulet hung beneath his shirt. And into the boiling, brimming scene!

"You're playing as if you don't believe they're even there," Yan disrupted the commotion. "Did you think they'd up and gone? Can't you hear their constant quacking?"

At the welcome voice, Toi rested the stick to the ground. Not until it leaned on his shoulder did he pull down the blindfold and gaze Yan's way, his first words between theatric pants.

"No, not really…I only really…hear yours…"

"Okay, I'm only piping in because I noticed someone's egg about to totter right off his shoulders."

"And when exactly did you start taking such an interest in other people's eggs, Mother Goose?"

"Ever since I've had to endure the stink that seeps out that crack in yours!"

Maybe because the others had come to expect a more sadistic entertainment in Toi and Yan's not uncommon repartees did they unconsciously relent their own cruel sport. Even the blood-thirstiest of bullies can appreciate a bloodless bout when there's this much sharp-tongued zeal. Yet the joke was on them, for it was indeed an act these two were staging, improvising in turn like a pair of comedians in tune with one another's repertoire and style. And every one of those five vicious morons was eating it up.

"Now that's a laugh, coming from the very baby chick I spied last night, wingtips between his drumsticks, cheep-cheep-cheeping away!" Toi countered with, embellishing the accusation with a rather lewd pantomime. And on went the two in turn, heaping insult upon insult, gesticulating wildly back and forth, as if they were unaware of the crowd of folks gathering about.

At last Toi seized the golden opportunity and raised his stick as if to strike. Yan read the cue and dashed away full sprint, Toi right behind hollering something horrible yet unintelligible.

The others stood and watched this strange finale receding down the distant sidewalk. What could any of the abandoned audience have done or said? The entire production, which turned out to be nothing more than a disappearing act, had long since reached such a level of absurdity, no one knew what to even ridicule now that it was finished.

*

Toi caught up to Yan behind a magazine stall. Each smiled a familiar smile. Toi tossed his stick onto a pile of newspapers and began unknotting the kerchief from his throat. The stall-keeper peered back over his shoulder at the boys and crinkled his downy moustache in tacit disapproval. This provided them extra amusement.

"Mother Goose? Did I seriously call you that?" Toi laughed. "What took you so long?"

"I was sure you'd get out alive without me for once," Yan teased as they crossed the road. They continued up the opposite walkway, the one delighting each time he snatched his rescuer's shy but level glance. Despite their similarity in size, Toi was a couple years his best friend's wiser.

He did however seldom mind the gap since his was the venerable position of mentor. And yet this irreverent tone Yan was assuming lately, it was something altogether different. Toi was pleased with his understudy's blossoming spunk. It was flattering too in a way. Yan hadn't always been so brave.

When they'd started hanging out, it took Toi quite some time to coax him out from under his shell. Toi remembers how he first found Yan, only five at the time, concealed in a bush with his nose in a comic book during recess. The shrub he'd chosen to hide in reeked of urine because he'd wet his school pants and was trying to buy enough time for the stain to evaporate. "That'll dry faster in the sun," Toi introduced himself with.

It didn't take the lot of bullies long at all to hone in on easy prey like Yan. Sharks to blood. It was like an irrevocable curse that had been building all throughout Yan's childhood. Which is why Toi stepped in so precipitately, and with more than just the usual zeal to defend one in need. Someone had to teach the child how to protect himself, how to stand up for his own beliefs. Toi had to admit that Yan turned out to be nearly as smart as he himself had been at that age. But there was something so innately sensitive, so thoughtful and genuine, noble too, Toi could never quite say what it was that'd fascinated him from the start.

As far as Toi was concerned, all of this was a plain matter of survival. These elaborate charades were simply his means of proving his superiority, no matter how his idiotic classmates might see things otherwise. The only way he could have relished the moment more was if there'd been some pretty girls about to witness.

The two leaned against the wall of an office building in the day's full sun. Toi pulled out a half-smoked cigarette he'd spotted someone drop that morning before class and offered the find to his friend. Yan took it and shoved it in his pants pocket and probably planned to trash it. Too bad, thought Toi, who wished it'd been refused so he could calm his nerves and smoke it later in private. Oh hell, those five neighborhood brutes wouldn't be so damn insufferable if they weren't so damn narrow.

"I see you've still got that charm around your neck. Don't think it's going to do you any good," Toi admonished. Yan wondered if he'd said something to upset him.

They stood there silently for a spell watching the traffic pass. Yan felt he owed something more sincere in reply but couldn't sense how to go about it.

"Does your mom still want you to do it?" he finally asked.

Toi's mother had insisted he pledge to become a monk in honor of the recent funeral. She'd pestered him about it every awful step up to the cremation. The memory of her scornful glare still twinged in his brain for not getting up and shaving his head during the ceremony. Later that night she told him his sister's spirit would haunt him till the day he died.

"Me? Can you imagine? Initiate Toi! There's no way I'm letting go this lion's prize," vigorously rubbing his unruly mane of hair. Yan laughed, but out of force of habit. Toi could see his companion was withdrawing again.

"You never let me bash any brains out. I never get to taste their blood," he rekindled Yan's affections with one last shared smile.

Chapter 3: The Work

Toi loved to catch up on what Yan'd managed to add during class each day, he loved to take the notepad home at night and giggle over its latest content under sheet by flashlight. It was then his habit to return it next morning with some facetious yet invested comment concerning the comic's current state of affairs and where he thought it ought to venture next. When one notepad filled, Toi would store it with the others, then buy Yan another. This simple back and forth ritual brought both the boys the greatest pleasure.

Yan and Toi of course got top billing. More accurately it was Great Detective Yan and his guardian the preeminent Doctor Toi who did. For the compass of their adventures was rarely more than a thinly disguised plagiary of the Japanese serial of obvious influence. And while Toi personally felt his own real-life exploits merited more literary attention, he was nevertheless honored to have been elected Yan's fictional mentor as well. The story's overarching premise went something like this (again, forgiving the innumerable similarities with the work's manga inspiration):

> Detective Yan, once a strapping, prodigal youth of seventeen, undergoes a fantastical reversal when the sinister Dark Matters Agency slips him a dragon fruit dosed with an experimental mind-control serum. The DMA's ploy fails, but not without unforeseen side-effects. The drug makes the adolescent regress a decade or more in age. Now fearing for his forever-altered life, the lad goes into hiding under the tutelage of his childhood companion's father, Doctor Toi. The sage doctor immediately recognizes his understudy's uncanny smarts and puts it to its destined and most honorable use—to cracking the world's greatest unsolved crimes.

From here caper after outlandish caper could readily unravel. Many were admittedly torn right from the pages of the press, so to speak. Others acquired more of a local flavor: *The Mystery of the Krasue*; *Ravana's Revenge*; etc. But when it came down to picking favorites, the episodes that brought Toi the widest smiles were those immortalizing the cast of characters that populated their daily lives. There was for starters Professor Nagani, who had inherited the unfortunate role of arch-nemesis in Yan's catalog. Yan always emphasized the professor's thick eyebrows that twitched from page to page like two angry caterpillars intimating the evilest of intent. The real Nagani had no clue, though he was hardly the only one getting poked fun at. There was Yan's older cousin, her wildly dyed hair warranting an exclusive use of color. She'd absolutely kill them both if she ever found out about the idiotic shit her little cousin made her comic book persona say and do. Or take Toi's own character who wore that silly monocle, which made him look like some pompous British scholar. Toi admired the way the doctor kept his hallmark spectacle in place during the most action-packed of scenes. Yan did abruptly drop the unfortunate storyline where Toi's mom had been plotting the doctor's death. It was replaced with some other little bit of scribbled distraction. Not ever having intended any harm.

Yan's draftsmanship could only be classified as naïve, which isn't to say he didn't have some envisioned ideal of excellence, and only on behalf of the smallest of audiences. Toi ever proved the faithful critic. Only once had he brought up the exaggerations of Yan's caricatures, though he never mentioned the wayward paths of his restless lines and swirls. He did though often remark on how he admired Yan's *Profundity of Shadows*, as if he'd been encouraging the young Rembrandt van Rijn himself. And having gotten beyond the artist's love for ink, Toi had to admit there was a counterbalancing spartanness to all other forms of narrative device. The heavy-handed gestures that stumbled the action from frame to frame never revealed anything subtler than physical movement through space; characters pandered to their own worst stereotypes; dialogue was distilled to its meekest necessity; plotlines kept stealing from and contradicting themselves over and again. Really, what wasn't there for Toi to relish? For each horrendously realized page was a blessed celebration of every childish prank he ought to be too old for. The others, those jackasses back on the street, they'd humiliate him to no end if they knew about his reading tastes. But within the pages of Yan's comic book, that little stupid boy inside of Toi could still exist and without fear. In the ridiculous guise of a monocled medic.

Night after night Toi returned to that imagined, pleasantly frozen realm. And he'd damned near laughed himself right to sleep most of them.

*

Neither boy once thought it odd that, throughout the close to eight years they'd shared this secret ritual, Yan's fictional sleuth never aged the least. Time itself could not distort the great detective. It was as if he were somehow the immutable embodiment of his own reliable catchphrase: "One truth alone!"

Lately though each on their own began to wonder if something obvious wasn't missing.

Chapter 4: Actaeon, Actaeon

For the last day now, Fah was the only good reason for attending class, at least as far as the male half of the student body was concerned. She'd just moved to the city from the outskirts of Chiang Rai. Her mannerisms and her accent, well those were the epitome of an upcountry upbringing—that's what her new classmates mocked most behind her back. And while there was something grating about Fah's bumpkin ways to all those urbane girls born and raised in Bangkok, there was something conversely exotic to the opposite sex. Still, any girl unfortunate enough to witness the wave of manly posturing could see right through to those schoolboys' hopeless terror before this strange girl's penetrating gaze. One look from Fah was all it took, and you knew she knew it. This new girl—she sure didn't behave like she was new. She affected none of the modesty one surely ought to expect.

Maybe it was those stubby pigtails, how she wore them high and slightly tilting forward, like horns, that put her instantly at odds with many of the others. Yan however felt that, combined with the broad aquiline nose and those lively eyes, the pigtails made her look more like a falcon flaring its wings in warning. She was so sinewy and strong compared to the rest of her gender and age. Certainly her voice, which Yan had only heard say "Yep" when roll was called in geography class this morning, would eventually reveal all the inevitable sweetness hidden beneath. No one else Yan was confident enough to query had dared to try and speak to her. If only to elicit but a couple words from this mesmerizing creature once and for all, but under what pretense? How to ensure that Toi wouldn't show up and frighten her off with all his tireless jesting?

*

When Yan approached, Fah was alone, leaning upon the edge of the courtyard's fountain, washing some juice from the corner of her smile with a handful of its still, greenish water. So magnetic was the image of her wiping the drips from her chin with one long finger and thumb, Yan froze to. There was something strangely ashen about her skin, marmoreal. It was like stumbling upon the statue of a bathing goddess in the jungle, or so it seemed just then. Might he but watch unnoticed—yet when her eyes did snare him, both his and her different sorts of smiles vanished. Those pigtails suddenly were sharp and menacing, very horn-like indeed. Yan was too timid to let her see him reach to the amulet hid beneath his shirt.

"It'll come off easier with soap," he ventured, and brought at least his own small smile back.

"I recognize you. You're the one who thought Melbourne was in Australia this morning in geology class."

Yan was not about to correct her on either error.

"That was me…I mean, it's true, it *is* me."

"Truuuuuuly?" she sustained mockingly. At least her smile had returned too, if only for its own sole benefit. Yan stood silent, visibly embarrassed. Fah was the first to break the awkward interval.

"So are you important around here or anything?" drying her grin with the collar of her school shirt. Her accent mellowed the question—the pop-exam actually—with a conciliatory mischievousness. The juice was gone from her mouth, but now she'd stained her shirt with lipstick. Yan felt utterly dumb. He tried to think of what Toi would say, who always knew how to command the conversation, even when a girl was involved. Yan answered with the most pretentious thing he could conjure.

"I hate to blow my own horn, but I sort of like to think of myself as …" he started, putting one foot up on the fountain's rim for effect. For some reason Fah winced suddenly at his words…or maybe it was the mysterious rogue shadow that suddenly crossed the fountain's water which made her flinch. "…something of an…" Yan continued, unaware.

And here! Here his self-declaration was cut tragically short by the jarring rubbery *POING* of a red playground ball ricocheting off the back of his head! He bit into the tip of his tongue and shouted out (it must be noted) one particularly specific word. The ball then plunked into the water, splattering the crotch of his pants. Blind still with the pain throbbing between his teeth, beneath Fah's uncontrollable laughter, Yan heard Toi's silver-fanged words slithering in upon the scene.

"Watch your tongue, toilet-mouthed child! You could have soaked the lady with a stunt like that! Is that how you welcome our new peer? Is this how you welcome this beautiful young lady...? Let me introduce myself," Toi shifted his attention. "My name is Toi. And you of course are Fah. Everyone's been talking..."

Yan couldn't tell which Toi was shoveling on more thickly: the insults or the flattery. It was although quite clear the compliments were hardly disingenuous. In an effort to salvage some shred of honor, Yan instinctively assumed the prescribed role, to meet Toi on the battlefield he had picked.

"Forgive my classmate's aim. His family suffers from a medical history of Wandering Ball Syndrome," Yan rallied, still rubbing behind his ear. The retort turned Fah's smile to his favor.

"It's obvious to me and Fah both," Toi struck back fast, indicating Yan's doused pants, "that this is *exactly* how lowdown you'll dare to tread!"

Toi had probably underestimated Fah. Yan was well within his rights to defend himself.

"Oh, I'm not so sure so obvious," and here she rose. "But I'll see you in geography tomorrow, sugar," she whispered directly to Yan in leaving.

People don't call other people 'sugar' unless they mean something! Toi must not have heard. And yet, as he and Yan watched her walk off, each too thunderstruck to notice the other's oblivion, was there any doubt that Fah had in the end crowned Yan the victor?

"She is just something else! Something sterling!" Toi gushed, plying his friend to acknowledge the indisputable truth behind his statement.

"She's not the only one."

"Those pants of yours will dry faster in the sun," Toi sarcastically offered. He was sure Yan didn't know yet about the blood that'd been dripping down his chin throughout the whole scene, making him look like something of a moronic, pants-wetting vampire.

Chapter 5: An Early Study in Pink

Yan completely skipped all the usual destinations that afternoon. He did not linger along the school gates to eavesdrop on the clans of girls gossiping just outside. That day he did not scan the street stall tables of comics for the latest releases. Nor did he offer to help with small jobs outside Toi's father's restaurant for a few baht to blow at the Wanco Gingko minimarket. Nor, in truth, did he sketch. Professor Nagani had finally snatched the notepad when Yan was looking over it during class. And besides, Toi never asked for it back today.

Yan began to entertain the conclusion that the only way he might ever have but one untainted moment alone with Fah again was if he could avoid running into Toi for the rest of his life. Well maybe at least for the rest of the day. What would he even say to her? It didn't matter.

Yan did although eventually run into his cousin, Pink. Pink had a bag from the mall in hand, which she discreetly moved behind her back when she spotted him. Pink wasn't sure why she felt like she had anything to hide, but she did.

Nonetheless she had a distinct psychological edge over her little cousin. Not only did Pink know his mother forbade him to talk to her, she was moreover a seasoned teenager. Oh and yes, her hair was pink.

"Little brother, why the forlorn stare? It's not your usual one."

"Leave me alone. This once...please."

Pink knew Yan wanted quite the opposite, so she took his arm in hers, smiling only somewhat condescendingly. The sound of the traffic thinning along Chit Lom swelled and faded over them in waves as they walked on quietly for some while.

"It's nothing you'd be able to help with anyways. Nothing you'd understand," Yan finally broke their silence.

"It's a girl then. Do you know how silly that sounds? You needn't say another word." Yan caught all three of his cousin's implications: 1) the cause of his melancholy was obvious; 2) she certainly did know how to deal with such things; and 3) Yan had better zip it if he knew what was good for him. He interrupted nonetheless.

"She's no ordinary girl. Fah's more than just a girl." This explanation was getting him nowhere. "I don't know... she's impossible. I mean unsolvable. I don't think Toi would even know quite how to handle Fah." He cringed at having slipped and uttered his friend's name in the same breath.

Pink, for her part, never thought the less about Toi anymore, especially since that overconfident windbag had finally given up on flirting with her. And she felt bad for him in light of recent events. Besides, who else was going to look out for her little cousin when she wasn't around?

"Listen, Toi's no better at this game than you are. Look at the sort of half-wits he chases after lately. Trust me, you should stop obsessing over some stupid conquest and start thinking more about yourself. You're way too young to be bowing before the first girl to stroll around the corner."

"I told you you'd refuse to understand."

"Stop yourself right there!" Pink's smile fell like a stone knocked from the roof. "If you think yours is the only deluded heart to've wept itself to sleep, then the rest of humanity may have a bone to pick with you. If there's a drop of reason left in that love-sick skull of yours, admit you're hardly the first. Whether you want to or not, you're going to have to survive!"

Yan resented the sound admonishment for sullying the ideal he was trying to construct. Yet he allowed it the time it deserved to sink in.

"Really? Must I really?" he resigned at last. Pink read his reluctant smirk as a sign of triumph.

"Yes, you idiot!" she laughed in way of goodbye when they'd reached the front of his building. Yan held onto that parting image, of how her smile warmed as he turned away, like a genuinely concerned cousin's should. Once the door had closed behind, he had to confess he did feel a tiny better.

Pink continued on her way, poking her nose back into her bag to admire the bra she'd splurged on, it too being pink. And thus so fancifully did the memory of this encounter with her cousin almost wholly flee. Not once had Pink suspected, nor would she ever, that the type of girl she'd vilified as a 'half-wit', the precise girl she'd seen earlier that afternoon with Toi at a street-stall buying sweet-treats, had actually been Fah.

Chapter 6: The Nightmare

"Mother?" Yan called out though he well knew she wasn't home. But there was still a quick meal lovingly prepared and waiting, warm in a couple pots upon the table. Yan grabbed fork and spoon hastily. Spicy and sweet, the way the mother knew her son liked it. The moment he finished, he washed his dishes and went to bed.

The sun had dropped low and silhouetted the delicate foliage of the tamarind tree outside his and his mother's room. The lights were off, and night's cool draft began to float through the open window like an invisible mist. Yan lay with his feet sticking out of the sheets, letting the sounds of the streets fade beneath his thoughts, staring up at the darkening ceiling, as if something was starting to brew there on that familiar grey tableau.

The one same tortuous thought resurfaced over and over in his mind. What an ass he'd been. Who had he been pretending to be at the time? As much as he hated to have to admit it, Toi wasn't exclusively to blame.

Toi hadn't been any bigger of a jerk than he, or Fah for all that. But Yan could've prevailed by refusing to play the counterpart. Without any of the habitual charade, he could have easily presented his truer self. Yan pondered for a while what might be his *truer self*, and he couldn't quite picture it without also picturing Toi. Oh god, he could barely believe he'd even been there to experience it, so strange were the images left flashing inside his brain. It was as if he'd been drugged at the time, or like some spell had been controlling his body throughout. Something more sinister than the dirty trick with the ball had been at the heart of the episode earlier that afternoon. Something dire perhaps and immutable.

The tamarind swelled on a graceful breeze as its feathery leaves grew crisp and intricate in the rising full moon. The moon's light gently blotted Yan's drowsing vision through and through.

*

When he awoke, it was nighttime yet. But everything was silent, dead silent.

Never in its eternal life has Bangkok been silent.

All Yan could hear was the tamarind rustling in a waft of air. He put on his pajama pants and descended from his room.

The flat of his feet thudded unnaturally audibly on the cement stairs in the noiselessness that permeated both inside and out. When he stepped onto the street, it was deserted, not a soul in sight. The quiet was mind-blowing. The city lights were only half-lit , unchanging, unmoving. All the cars or motorbikes were parked and vacant. The shops were closed, all the apartment windows curtained black. Come to think of it, Yan couldn't even hear his neighbor snoring, and that old fart snored throughout any fucking calamity the night might bring. What time could it be?

Yan looked up to the heavens. The moon had flown. Instead, above the dim city, the whole fiery dome of stars glared down as if to plummet, lance-like, upon the vast abandoned metropolis. Upon Yan and Yan's soul alone. The stars' light pricked into every nerve along his skin. An overpowering physical sensation of the here-and-now— of this one-and-only here-and-now—the incomprehensible mental impression of standing beneath the brilliant night sky in a city utterly devoid of life, tingled up the back of his neck to the crown of his head. This was no dream, but what other realm? Why was he of all people chosen to be here? Was there something he was meant to do?

Who can describe the emotions tussling in Yan's heart as he mustered the courage for that next step out into this deserted kingdom?

Through an almost pure superstition he followed in reverse down the walk he and Pink had taken earlier that evening, trying to recall what their precise steps had been. Past the same seafood restaurant. Underneath the same scaffolding clinging to an office front. Past the stalls on the corner of Petchburi. Over the raised cement walkway spanning over, if only to stay true to the path he and his big cousin had taken, though there was no traffic to avoid now.

Can you imagine, as he explored the empty streets, his understandable terror mixed with excitement, eventually mixed with curiosity, and at last playfulness? And next a resiged internal laugh (for none would dare release an actual laugh into that silence) at the absurdity of the situation. Then a sort of creeping mania. Finally a good old-fashioned dose of sentimentality and loneliness. Surely anyone could feel all these at once in the face of such. The city and the night seemed to extend endlessly before him. It is difficult to know how quickly and how often such thoughts surfaced and submerged as he inched his way along. If only there was another, just one other here to mark the miracle.

When he reached the canal, Yan stopped halfway across the bridge to gaze below. He found the waves' lapping against the banks unexpectedly mesmerizing since there was no din with which to compete tonight. The pitch water was visually defined by the dancing reflection of the starry sky above, which the canal seemed to contain and mollify. The splashing began to measure out Yan's own heartbeat, which calmed to match its natural pulse undisturbed by the usual water traffic. He closed his eyes and felt the sound carry him back somewhere older than the city, to somewhere more native and unchanging. It was difficult for him to have to leave the sanctuary of that water's unchallenged song.

Still emerging from this daydream, as he descended the stairs at the other side, he thought he heard a footstep upon the bridge behind. He looked back nervously, saw no one and, after a moment's stillness, wrote it off to nothing more than a heightened sense of paranoia.

He paused a minute beneath the looming BTS station, just to make sure a train wasn't going to pass. Here was the end of his reenacted trek. This was about where he had run into to his cousin earlier that day. He was tempted for a moment to explore the enormous malls to the east, but decided their emptiness might turn out to be unbearably eerie. So Yan continued south through the areas designed to be, at least under normal city circumstances, slightly quieter and less populated. Tonight this hardly mattered, except perhaps in the psyche of the solitary, where the dead silence of the streets seemed less ominous the less relatively barren they now were. It was a long and often dark walk down Soi Lang Suan, to no known purpose.

Eventually Yan reached the edge of Lumpini Park. At first the lush gardens beyond the outer tree line looked weirdly more foreboding than the vacant cityscape he'd grown accustomed to. But a little outward giggle at the NO DOGS ALLOWED posted at the entryway eased him enough to suppose it was probably safe within.

He sensed a distinctly different atmosphere the moment he stepped upon the footpath. The streets had seemed indifferent to his existence; something inside the park though seemed to invite.

It was like a glass case had been placed around the entire grounds. Yan inhaled deeply and was reinvigorated by the vaporous, almost living breath. The tension in his muscles relaxed and he realized how sore his feet had become from all the walking. His eyes had grown heavy too and Yan began to wish he'd never left his bed. Yet his legs lugged forward still, at least up into the grass where his toes cooled themselves a while. When he reached the park's immense pond, unconscious to the sound of the waves repetitively licking its shore, he felt he must sit down. The earth was damp beneath his bum.

How long did he sit there staring into that liquid body? So rapt in thought was he, he no longer noticed the reflection of the shifting stars as they dimmed behind the kindling light of approaching day. Nor did he see the waning sliver of moon, with its bright companion planet, start to rise upon the coloring waters beneath the central dock where the boats were moored. A stupefying weariness, as that of opium-induced slumber, now deadened his senses.

What if he were trapped inside this nightmare forever? Yan began to miss his cousin. He missed Toi and craved his guidance. And Fah. What if he was meant to never gaze upon Fah again? The idea welled inside his throat, and he almost began to cry. Above all, Yan missed his mother.

And it was then that the bell first rang, far off.

Hidden in a nearby tree, some birds snapped into flight above Yan's head. As the quivering flock swerved swiftly across the pond and their fading rush of sound disappeared into the darkness, the bell echoed again.

A sudden horror seized our dreamer, who'd previously believed himself universally alone. Again it rang, then again. The buildings towering over the trees seemed to rumble with and funnel each subsequent clang closer toward Yan's vulnerable sanctuary, each time louder and encroaching more fiercely! Yan scurried into a thicket of ferns and crouched within. What demon was striking the maddening tones, on and on?

But then it stopped.

As the final metallic cry was still decaying in his ears, Yan heard his own heartbeat. He clutched his hand to his chest to muffle it, feeling the cool amulet he wore about his neck pulse between his ribcage and his palm, trying to stay very still beneath a broad palm frond from which he peeked. Nothing. No more sound. Danger had passed. Morning would soon be here. If he could stay safely concealed just a little longer. If only he'd thought to pee...

There came a wind-like rustle across the lawn and a shadow congealed from out of nothing before Yan's eyes. The hunched, almost inhuman form prowled toward his hiding place methodically, like a snake crazed with starvation.

Now Yan knew why he had been lured here. Now he could hear the creature's snarl, see its hideous yellow teeth. There was no mistaking: he had been spotted—he'd been identified! This unholy incarnation had hunted him down!

An unnatural thrill galvanized the boy's brain and limbs! If he was to survive, he must spring upon and strangle his friend before the coming of the full daytime light!

Chapter 7: The DNA

In a separate corner of Bangkok quite removed from Lumpini Park, and long beyond the hour of dawn, buried inside an enormous building known simply as 'Center Office', Mr Torpong was putting paperwork in order. It was his paperwork: no one else's ever crossed the threshold of that solitary office. The documents came daily in well-worn manila envelopes through a slot in his door at about knee-level. And every time, after the parcel thudded to the floor, Mr Torpong muttered out something like, "Good day, thank you." The anonymous deliverer on the other side either never heard, or didn't care to respond. At the end of each shift, it was his custom to deposit the forms tucked back inside their envelope into a basket near reception. He assumed it was that same young secretary behind the desk there with her nose in a magazine who would bring a fresh batch the next morning. Torpong was beginning to resent those brightly manicured hands of hers, especially because the packets had been coming by twos and threes and fours lately.

So unaccustomed was Mr Torpong to this recent flood, he couldn't decide where to start with this morning's daunting stacks. So he scrunched them into a single messy pile which he finally removed from sight behind a conveniently large potted palm. He slumped into his chair and swiveled back and forth in distracted rhythm, staring into the thicket of that overgrown houseplant, trying to recall if he'd been the one who brought it in or if the plant been here from the first. The untouched mug of tea on his desktop was going tepid.

Though his solemn round face hardly betrayed it, he was growing increasingly anxious the closer the appointed hour approached, for a time had been appointed. Mr Torpong was awaiting a call, a conference call no less. Not in his twelve years at the post had he participated in a conference call. And to make matters worse, he knew that, at some point during this intimidatingly novel experience, he was going to have to relay something significant, something possibly upsetting to a faceless audience of bigwigs up the bureaucratic food-chain.

Our Mr Torpong's own professional rung was rather low. You see, he worked for the Distinguished Nebulae Agency and did in fact comprise its total staff. As one might guess from the department's title, the job must have pertained in some degree to meteorology. And if rumors are to be listened to, the qualifier 'Distinguished' was in fact the vestige of an ancient royal appointment. Mr Torpong however was not the sort to put himself in the path of pointless rumors. Besides, the office had long since technically devolved into an insignificant metropolitan post.

But let's not be too quick to judge. Would an upstanding employee like Mr Torpong ever devote a whole career to work that's only ever meant to be overlooked? Sooner or later someone was bound to take notice of all the paperwork getting accomplished. Indeed sooner arrived, well, sooner than later. To Torpong's surprise, an intimate group of influential city officials had recently taken an interest in the agency's output without ever really explaining its potential. As far as Torpong was concerned, this was sufficient proof that even in the most trifling of local government affairs, beauty remains in the eye of the beholder.

The phone rang and that little red light on its console finally flashed. He let the hand piece rattle a half time more before plucking it straight up.

"Thank you, good day, Commissioner. Okay, then let me thank you for your time," he blurted out and in fact bowed here halfway to the mouthpiece. "Then my message made its way to your esteemed desk?"

"To you too, Mr Torpong. Yes, of course," the smooth voice came through. "Now what is this you mention about faulty imaging?"

"Well, sir, our problem is with one of the nighttime scans."

"What is it? Image distortion?" the commissioner interrupted.

"Not exactly. It's a cloud, sir, over one of the sectors. Not a big one." Mr Torpong thought for a moment how he had never actually met the man on the other end face-to-face.

"Is it obstructing something important?"

"Oh no, nothing of the sort. It's just that the cloud in the image wasn't really there." This wasn't how Mr Torpong had planned segueing into his report.

"What do you mean? Is it there or isn't it? Then it is faulty imaging!" The commissioner was growing irritated.

"No, I promise. The equipment is fine. I've checked and double-checked the process logs and couldn't find a single flag," Mr Torpong reassured proudly. He had in fact triple-checked. His devotion was commendable, with neither wife nor family to distract him from the job.

There was a pregnant pause. And then an unknown voice intruded. It was a woman's. Mr Torpong had been so engrossed in his role, he forgot the crucial fact this was a conference call. But it wasn't him she was talking to. "I think he needs to have his eyes examined," she mumbled. A rush of shame flushed Torpong's cheeks and, like an accused schoolboy, he felt compelled to exonerate himself.

"I...I was there," he tried to address her, uncertain if his voice was getting through. "I was looking up at the stars last night. You see, I'm something of an amateur astronomer. There's never much to see in the city, light-pollution and such. The viewing's so much better in the mountains. But last night, for some reason the sky was so unbelievably clear last night. You could see constellations Bangkok hasn't seen in ages." Torpong thought he'd better get back to the crux of the matter. "Well, it's just I'd remember if there'd been a cloud in the sky at that moment," attempting to corroborate what he knew to be the truth, trying to round each word with a sense of modest probity.

There was another pause. He thought he heard the commissioner beg beneath his breath, "Sounds an honest sort at heart." Then the line hung up. And for some while after, poor Torpong just sat there wondering who he'd displeased. To whom had he dared direct this apparently objectionable answer?

Chapter 8: Blind Morning

It was the sound of his mother closing their front door that broke him from sleep. Blurry eyes just opening from their slumber might not even suspect they've missed something worth seeing.

Yan's thoughts went straight to Fah, of her as if frozen in his memory by the fountain again. Yan lay in bed a while longer in order to analyze the idea, like one savors the scent of an unknown spice that starts to heat inside a pan outside one's window. The fantasy's cloud was too aromatic. Not one of last night's particulars, no general impression from last night's dream troubled Yan's memory now. It had, as they say, been wiped off the face of this earth, off the face of his conscience, as dreams are so apt to do.

*

Yan expected to run into Toi on the way to school. At least that'd been his apprehension all morning. He considered playing sick to stay home. Let's face it, his feelings were still hurt, though time had worn down anger's edges until it resembled something more like shame, which is easier to mask.

Outside the stubborn light of day seemed to insist today was the only chance to reconcile yesterday's losses. Yan understood that, if he didn't act soon, he was going to lose Fah to that tedious series of handsome dumbshit-after-dumbshit of which their school had no shortage. But the more he played out the potential consequences in his mind, the more his confidence shriveled. It was too late though to turn back home: he'd made it all the way to school despite the menacing gust of thoughts.

But just when he crossed the gate into the courtyard, two strong arms suddenly seized him from behind, his throat clutched in their unyielding grip. The crushing strength was so slender, so smooth. That skin—it was Fah's skin! She smooshed her cheekbone hard into his face and puckered a devilish kiss into the air before him. Yan didn't know how to answer that wild, inscrutable smile.

"I've been waiting for you! Where were you last night?" she shouted into his ear. Yan's eyes darted wildly about to see if anyone was noticing this totally inappropriate, totally exhilarating, yet physically awkward accosting.

"Something up, sugar?" The return of this imperious term of endearment as she finally let Yan free upended him even further.

"Nothing, Fah, nothing," he stuttered, whose *nothings* said anything but. The unconvincing way in which he'd spoken her name, he had absolutely no idea what tone she expected. Yet here she stood, a hairsbreadth before him, his love idol, smiling and talking, her eyes gleaming deeply into his, as if she knew him perfectly well, indeed adored him intimately. How should one react when a wave of longed-for affection comes crashing down upon you like a tropical downpour?

"Those skinny chicken legs of yours best skip to class before Nagani catches us again," Fah teased warmly. Yan's heart told his arms to steal another embrace. His legs however heeded Fah's advice, because his head was still so shocked and scared. After all, he'd never been kissed before. Well, almost kissed.

*

Master Nagani's class was utterly surreal that morning. Until today, it'd been nothing but mind-numbingly dull.

Whatever the professor was prattling on about made no sense to Yan. Not that the content was tough to grasp, for Mr Nagani had nothing more complex to relay than an announcement of the lesson plan and the start of roll call. It was more of an audible phenomenon bedeviling Yan, who couldn't comprehend a single word his teacher spoke. The sounds seemed to ripple and reverberate about the walls like a swarm of fish caught in a whirlpool. The morning sun plunged its rays into the classroom window, as through a liquid prism, and sweat began to bead his brow as his eyeballs floated dizzily in their sockets. He felt as if the entire class was staring right at him, right through him. Could they see on his face the flashes of delight and the shadows of doubt that pulsed upon the inside of his skull like the flicker of a candle in the pelting rain?

What was the cause, what was the secret of Fah now perfectly smitten with him? Yan rifled every scrap of memory in hope of uncovering the key, of finding somewhere in the minute history of their acquaintance that critical yet heretofore unrecognized link between yesterday's fiasco and today's irrational bliss.

Then it was just a vicious joke. What a fool! And yet, though he couldn't penetrate the meaning of Fah's smile still blazing in his mind, Yan felt he could trust that one thing more than any of his doubts. Those eyes, those kindling eyes of hers concealed no lie. Then it was love! There was no other logical explanation except that Fah had somehow fallen in love! He marveled over the very ease of it at apparently so little cost.

"Petch?"

"Here, master," Petch answered.

"Pim?"

"Here, master," Pim answered.

Nagani was still calling roll. Yan's agony had lasted but a couple minutes. The list of names floated into his ears like a mermaid's mesmerizing, incomprehensible chant.

"Yan? Yan!"

"Yes," he finally heard himself reply. But had he actually spoken the word? It'd sounded so frail and distant.

"Okay then students, if you'll open up your books to chapter nine".

Wait, why? Why hadn't that other name been reached before his own, which was always the last? Why hadn't the professor called Toi's name? Where was Toi? Where was Toi's desk?

Chapter 9: The Eager Student

Yan looked around the edge of his book out the window at Fah sitting by the fountain. He knew she was waiting for him and that single idea terrified him. There was no one else in the classroom with him now except for Master Nagani at his desk. The other students had left for recess ten minutes ago. Every now and then the professor raised his head from his papers, rubbed the tired eyes beneath those bushy eyebrows and scrutinized his student incredulously. This boy had never shown an interest before in getting ahead with studies.

Once or twice Yan saw Fah peer toward his window, but he'd positioned himself so that he was concealed behind a diagram of the cell. When she'd avert her eyes again, he would lean forward slowly so that, from between the book and the diagram, he'd get a better look at the length of her body. There was something hypnotic in how, contrary to the rest of her almost stone-still torso, she rotated her head over her shoulder searching the courtyard. With every turn of her glance, her pigtails swayed like a pair of black dandelions with their fuzzy spheres of seeds dispersing on an impetuous wind. Yan's eyes traced the curved muscular line stretching, like a taught serpent, from the tip of her clavicle up the contour of her neck where it dissolved behind the jawbone. To think, it was him alone she was searching for. What did she expect him to do, expect him to be?

"Girl trouble, Yan?" Mr Nagani startled him. Yan returned the professor's dismissive gaze and then pretended to go back to reading. The clutter of words on the page were inclined to spin right off the paper.

"It's okay, you needn't say. I've seen it all before," Nagani closed the topic as quick as he'd raised it.

Just what could this old geezer possibly understand about Yan at this moment? What minutest particle of this uncanny universe into which he'd awoken could this insignificant man possibly fathom? As far as Yan was concerned, Professor Nagani was nothing more than a specter haunting a purely fantasy realm. Would you yourself, for even a second, begin to lend an ear to the platitudes of an annoying know-it-all figment of your trickster imagination?

For it was no longer all the world which Yan could see and hear and touch that plagued his thoughts. Rather it was the opposite of these illusory phenomena he found his mind submerging deep into. Like a massive stone tumbling through the center of his equilibrium, it was the silent, undeniable absence of his companion which began to eat him away from the inside.

Not once during class had a single person made reference to Toi. Nothing animate or inanimate suggested him having left a mark in this strange new place. It was as if, no matter where Yan turned, without a word or sound the whole earth was screaming in unison the nothingness that Toi now was. And none but he could hear to interpret that inaudible cry. How does one plead for an existence in a cosmos that unequivocally refuses that friend could ever have possibly been? No sign of Toi's antics upon the playground to rouse the crowd outside. Undoubtedly no cheated exam with his name among the pile the professor was presently drowning in ink.

Yan's heart sank to think of Toi as nothing more than an impalpable secret locked inside. Was Yan then even mentally sound enough, was his spirit worthy of that unfair task? He couldn't contain Toi, he could not, by himself, sustain all of what remained of Toi's faint meaning. What else can one call this sort of immateriality, what else to name this ghost whose survival depends on you alone—if not an angel? For Toi's now hidden predicament seemed dangerously akin to that same fragile tightrope between belief and doubt upon which the feet of the divine themselves must balance. What was to prevent Yan too from getting swallowed down whole into the

49

bargain? He began to question his ability to even endure what remained of this one particularly dismal day.

The school bell rang the end of recess and the children outside burst into a single motion like a flock of birds startled into flight. The silhouetted memory of Yan's dream returned in all its horrible implications.

And so he did remember, and a cloud of guilt rolled over his dimming thoughts. Did he yield the power? Could he have possibly been capable of erasing a life? The bell still toned as if it'd never cease. Yan's heart beat double. Blood pooled in the pit of his skull like a deadly arctic tide. He heard the rumble of the children's screams approaching and felt as if he were trapped in a collapsing underwater cavern. His head sunk into his tingling hands. Struggling to not black out, he drew what must've seemed like one last breath.

The school bell finished ringing.

His failing eyes lifted once more to Fah, who stayed by the fountain as the last students ran past her back to class. There she was, his only constant, Mae Khongkha herself. In one final grasp, all Yan's unraveling hopes wrecked onto this strange girl's inexplicable steadfastness like a castaway upon an island. And yet behold—an uncharted island of paradise! While there was something vital torn from his heart, from his now bizarrely cloven life, here too stood something born afresh, something equally profound and impenetrable. And instead it promised bliss! No sorrow, no loss…and no remorse.

His vision began to clarify. He watched her shift her weight from hip to hip and an electric shiver crackled through his spine to the tips of his billion nerves.

"If you boys spent half as much time studying as you do…"

But Nagani's student didn't catch the least of what he was lecturing on, because Yan had long since knocked his book onto the floor, took off without pushing in his chair, straight past the children scuffling in, and through the slamming classroom door into the open air.

Fah saw him quick and smiled. An uncontrollable light kindled in her smiling eyes, for it seemed to her as if a glorious aura emanated about the crown of Yan's head and poured over her from a heavenly angel. Yan, smiling too, came to Fah and, wrapping his arms about her, gave her a kiss upon her unhesitating, slightly parting lips. She wanted him to never let her go.

Chapter 10: Lunchtime Peripatetics

That whole rest of the morning Mr Torpong thought about heading out and had already eaten his noodles over his paperwork in anticipation of sacrificing the lunch hour for a lengthy walk.

Upon stepping out, his attention was not so much upon the metropolitan sound and fury per se that rings throughout the city at this particular time of day. The whirling shapes instead served merely like a photo album does to the traveler returning. Little lasting snippets here and there helped remind Torpong of specific circumstances from the previous night, like how a rogue evening breeze had rattled a spirit house he'd forgotten about. Or how that silent and majestic tamarind had dissolved into the skyline silhouette much as it will again in just another several hours. At least that was how he thought he remembered these things as he tried to recast them in last night's shadowier hue. But in the end such recollections seemed so prone to fading into the recesses of the past, scant strokes surviving on the surface of his consciousness, light as pastel on paper. He searched and searched, but found no object along his way that told more than a half-truth. How could he trust the memories they wanted to suggest?

Then he suddenly realized there was one thing though that had remained a constant, and right above his head this entire time: the immortal burning spiral of the starry sky. And while he could not actually see it now, in an abstracted sense he still could see it clearly.

Torpong periodically looked down at his wristwatch and then straight up to see if he couldn't mentally penetrate the vivid blue and place the stars veiled behind. He tried to picture the constellations' slow and noble rotation across the heavens. Much like a clockmaker's hand might stop a cog in motion, in his imagination he began to turn them and the hour itself into reverse. The blazing milestones of outer space danced backwards in his brain, faster through the vast machinery of the universe. He envisioned the sun, and then the crescent moon with the morning star sinking into the east, and then the morning light withdrawn. The assiduous black of night began to chisel out each the billion stars inside his intellect until— voilà the revealing spark! At last the lost and sought for instant. His position was exact. He had returned to the past that had, ever since, been summoning him back.

He was atop a bridge, which he'd reached almost as purblindly as a somnambulist. When Mr Torpong peered down into the waters of the small canal, it was not the actual waves rhythmically lapping its banks, but instead some sort of dreamlike reflection of the blazing celestial script in the moonless night that poured through our stargazer's memory and filled his very living eyes. Translucent now as night itself!

There couldn't have been a cloud in the sky last night, despite the images from some dumb weather satellite. Torpong was nearly sure that he'd seen otherwise. But in all honesty, he didn't recall the concrete proof. What had he seen reflected there in the waters that'd made him so damn certain?

Chapter 11: Wish I'd Never Known

If there was one thing that made Pink want to puke up her stomach-full of guts every time she had to see it, it was having to watch her little cousin and his new punk girlfriend drool over each other any given opportunity.

Hadn't she just finished publicly decrying "OMG", as read upon a couple dozen of her closest girlfriends' mobile phones, right before catching those two rabbits-in-heat at it again beneath the bridge over Klong Saen Sap. Oh god indeed! Yan's face was practically shoved right down that temptress's throat! Pink could barely endure gawking long enough to snap their picture.

The nauseating image she now studied on her phone conflicted so with her memories of the dorky prepubescent Yan of old, of that lonely boy who used to bring her worn-out comic books. That good-for-nothing Fah must have smelled her cousin's spotlessness right off the bat and seemed intent to poison it by making these exhibitions increasingly frequent and conspicuous.

Rumor was this wasn't the worst of what that little bitch fresh-off-the-farm liked sticking her big fat nose into.

Frankly there's no telling when it's a question of someone from the backwoods way up north. Pink nonetheless decided it wasn't wise to write Fah off entirely. Being alone in a new school, being plopped straight down into a whole new world could lead any girl to reckless measures.

As for her little cousin, well he was making a total jackass of himself. Why did he feel the need to publicly parade this recent rebelliousness? She even caught him smoking once and worried what he might let himself get talked into next. Or worse, Fah might trick him into undertaking something she was too clever to risk on her own. There was a time when Pink couldn't imagine the things her little cousin would come to do. Then again, she hadn't always been able to imagine all of what she herself had done.

Pink quickly deleted the photograph before she changed her mind.

Chapter 12: Slippery

The world becomes a slippery slope when all the universe's rules appear to sink beneath the earth on which you once so firmly stood. You start to think you've nothing to lose.

Yan peeked diffidently from around the corner of the Wanco Gingko minimart so that he could just make out the silhouette of the clerk counting money behind the register. He tried to act nonchalantly but could scarcely mask his anxiety. He had no idea what Fah's plan was. She told him to wait outside before sneaking in and behind the counter to steal the pack of cigarettes. Fah said he'd recognize his cue. What was taking so long? She'd walked in there like five minutes ago.

"MY GOD, I'M GONNA BURST!" Yan suddenly heard Fah scream from inside. The storekeeper jumped in alarm and blurted some half-unfinished expletive of concern. "I'M SAYING THIS THING'S GOTTA POP," Fah moaned on, and the man's shadow dashed from behind the counter and out of view.

Recognize his cue Yan did.

Yet Fah's melodramatic alarum did not foresee Yan's clumsy prowl forth getting intercepted with the simultaneous ingress of an old woman, whom he felt overwhelmingly obliged to bow to. The old grandma nearly had a heart attack halfway through the door Yan held open for her.

"A CURSE UPON MANKIND FOR THIS ANGUISH! AND ON YOU TOO, YOU OLD HAGS! FOREVER LURING VIRGINS INTO THIS WRETCHED BURDEN OF MOTHERHOOD WITH YOUR WICKED LIES!!!" Fah crowned the invective with, unleashing her con in every direction. Yan had to arch onto his tiptoes to see over the poor granny's trembling puff of hair before he spotted Fah pretending to writhe in pain on the floor, clutching her stomach, the owner dancing above her like a frightened mother hen. What did she have under her clothes that made her belly look so plump and bumpy? For fuck's sake, Fah was pretending she was pregnant and going into labor. But it was so stupidly obvious she'd stuffed a durian under her shirt. Yan froze, forgetting what he was supposed to do. "YOU USELESS LITTLE LUMPS OF..." Fah growled at her onlookers, her pigtails whipping wildly with each spastic roll upon the aisle. She then proceeded with unmistakable intent to kick over a stand of postcards for added effect. Yan couldn't but catch her scolding hint.

Cowering, he crept behind the counter and grabbed the closest thing at hand resembling a pack of cigarettes and shoved it into his pocket. He quickly scurried out the door, round the corner to the end of the alley, where he'd been told to wait, in the shadows now panting with excitement and praying Fah would get out okay. He began to fear he'd abandoned her to pay the price for their crime. Yan hoped that old lady survived.

"KEEP YOUR MITS OFF, PERVERT! DO YOU HAVE ANY IDEA HOW OLD I AM?" he heard Fah holler back over her shoulder as she came skipping around the corner, pulling the durian from under her shirt and holding it high above her head as if it were the trophy she'd coveted all along, and not the cigarettes. Yan's eyes lit up with a relieved and vanquished smile.

What did he need Toi for anymore?

Chapter 13: Messier Object 45. Several Stories One Evening

The possible deeper meaning of the mysterious cloud puzzled Mr Torpong on the walk back to the office and through the rest of his day. Plunged as he was again into the mountain of documents, he worked diligently so that whenever routine allowed, he might indulge the opportunity to further his personal investigation.

During afternoon break, he called a couple TV-station weathermen he knew. Or when he went to the supplies closet for another pen, he tried to chat about yesterday's sunset with the intern seated there. Or on his way into the bathroom, he nabbed the newspaper from reception in order to thumb through for any photographs of last night's sky. It was all just so much clutching after straws. Not one resource could either corroborate or refute his claim that the cloud did not exist. Perhaps he really did need his glasses checked. And so, come the end of his shift, he thought it best to leave it and the office all behind.

Outdoors a cool and kinder air diffused throughout the shadows filling Bangkok. At last Torpong's workday tension was beginning to relax from the exercise of walking home. Now that he'd finally dispelled the cloud from his mind, he felt capable of letting his tired thoughts float freely on the impressions that come from having to navigate the brisk and yet hypnotic rhythm of the streets. He indulged the fanciful musings that rose and mixed then fell inside his head with the steady coming of the eventide. What better really than this sort of unbound dreaminess when it comes to shaking off an enigma that, at first glance, seems unsolvable? What does the mind need more when it embarks upon imagination's carefree seas, if but a single star to steer her by?

When Torpong reached Victory Monument, he unthinkingly looked up.

There it was in the ageless sky—that well known cluster of stars, one of the few night-sky objects distinctly visible in the city's drowning man-made light. The Pleiades—the Seven Sisters. So honored among constellations, Athens itself aligned the Parthenon with their rising. They appear like just a smudge to the modern city-dweller, but to the trained eye, they're a delicate ring of glowing pearls, blurry and distant, yet so constant one feels they might be grasped.

Surely every reader has witnessed this heavenly septet before, even if you didn't realize its name or place in history at the time. And yet the thing the first-time observer notices first is their one glaring omission: except under the rarest of conditions, even the keenest can never make out more than six of the seven mentioned stars. Still almost all the myths insist there are the seven lights. There must have been epochs when the hidden one was not so faint.

We are all familiar with our national folktale of the six baby chicks that followed their mother hen's honorable march into the sacrificial flame, just so an old farmer couple might feed a monk passing through their neck of the jungle. Really, the tale sounds embarrassingly rustic by all comparison. (I've heard though that the Vikings tell a similar account.) One should although in passing note how the fated Greek sisters were not the only ones to find immortality among the heavens through suicide. Καταστερισμοί: catasterismi! That is what the Greeks called it. 'Being placed among the stars.' One can only imagine it to be an irreversible process.

The Babylonians called the cluster MUL.MUL....*star of stars*.

The Maori call them Matariki, perhaps translating 'eyes of god,' the name they also give to the season when the constellation first appears in the southern hemisphere.

But of all the designations this cluster enjoys, perhaps the holiest passed down derives from ancient Hinduism. Vedic astrology, which calls the celestial body the *Star of Fire*, teaches that the group is ruled by the great deity of the sacred fire: Agni the seven-tongued minister of ritual sacrifice and intercessor between man and the gods. And as the Mahabharata additionally informs, the stars themselves are said to represent Agni's offspring Murugan, who was conceived through Svaha's deceit and raised by the six wrongly incriminated wives of the Seven Sages. Svaha it was who gave birth to Lord Murugan the Six-faced, also known as Skanda, god of war and victory, whose roots dig as deep as an aboriginal Tamil nature idol. Murugan, whose temples extend from South Delhi to Sri Lanka, and to the Batu Caves outside Kuala Lumpur. Lord Murugan who is eternally young! He who is depicted upon a blue peacock, the Divine Spear in hand! Whose radiant visage removes all Darkness from this world! And on and on and...

This mythological sampling represents only a handful of the tales and texts, and it's exceedingly likely only portions were known to Mr Torpong. Sure, a dilettante stargazer can't help but getting his fingers dirty with a little of the 'local flavors'. These stories however were not what intrigued him most about this clump of stars in their special corner of the heavens. Torpong derived a far more gratifying sense of wonderment through studying the strictly scientific qualities of what astronomers call Messier object 45. Let's start with the basics.

The Pleiades is a relatively young open cluster roughly 100 million years old. We estimate it will survive another 250 million, around which time the pelting arm of our own Milky Way will exacerbate the cluster's ultimate dispersion. It is comprised mostly of hot blue stars accentuated by a nebula through which it's presently passing. Astronomers have statistically proven it to actually contain more than a thousand stars composing a core radius that stretches approximately eight light-years across. Their combined mass is thought to equal 800 of our suns. Any outside body will begin to disintegrate upon encroaching within a 43-light-year radius, which is the cluster's gravitational tidal limit.

Being roughly 120 parsecs = 391 light-years = 3.72 quadrillion kilometers away from Earth, it stands out as one of the closest of its kind, an attribute which has granted the Pleiades an illustrious position in the annals of astronomy. Both its proximity and plurality allow us, in a very elegant manner, to subsequently map the incomprehensible distances one encounters when exploring the depths of space. For you see, we can calculate our distance from the Pleiades through the simple trigonometric principle of the parallax. The measurement is solved thus: as the

Earth follows its orbit, the stars appear to converge and diverge, be it ever so minutely, throughout the cycle of a year. (Our planet is a moving observation point after all.) By measuring the same clustered group from different angles, by recording how far the Seven Sisters expand and contract in relationship to each other with our own charted planetary movement about the sun, we're able to solve their distance from our solar system.

And thus is forged the first rung upon which can be construed a limitless ruler. An Extragalactic Distance Scale. With this one mastered measurement, we can similarly in turn extend a golden standard to the next rung, and then the next, and reach into the furthest recesses of the cosmos. Perhaps to places never seen before—a veritable Jacob's ladder.

Mr Torpong had unwittingly wandered, head to the skies, right to the brink of traffic whirling around Victory Monument. A swirl of astronomical concepts danced in his head like a spirited breeze that made the silhouetted skyscrapers seem to sway, that made the bottomless hours of the nighttime feel so blown about and small.

It was then he felt a gentle brushing against the cuff of his pants, at first mistaken for the wake of a passing motorbike. Torpong looked down and saw it was instead a black-and-white cat, which must have been just about the only thing still left on Earth capable of distracting him from all of this heady business about the stars.

Chapter 14: The 42-story Spirit House

Yan didn't want to ask where Fah had obtained the money to take them in a tuk-tuk all the way down to the river. The driver looked at them incredulously when the young couple leapt unto the squeaky cushion, the durian fumbling in their laps. But Fah offered five extra baht up front. The tuk-tuk sputtered its way back onto the boulevard and soon into their ride a gentle mist fizzled throughout the humid night air. The streets and the hair on their heads glistened as if with a sheet of diamonds. Yan did not mind the rain, nor the consequent paralysis of traffic. He and Fah sat closely, holding hands, laughing childishly at each other's stupid jokes, and most of all trying to steal eager kisses whenever the driver was too preoccupied with driving. The only time the man did in fact glance back was when he caught whiff of the durian Fah sliced open with her pocketknife. The custard inside dripped down their fingers as they carefully licked clumps off the blade in turn. Where exactly was she taking him? Yan almost didn't care, so perfect was their romantic carriage ride.

"...Not half as idiotic as you looked when you saw me rolling on the floor about to give birth to our first-born son!" she mocked Yan affectionately. Who was this girl that was perfectly comfortable joking with him with such abandon? One thing he did know was that if it hadn't been for Fah, he would have never had the guts to steal. It was a marvel he was able to behave so boldly. Perhaps this is how it feels to become a man, for this is how Fah made him feel, though he had to admit he also felt a little guilty.

"How're you so sure it was going to be a boy?" he answered back. Fah's smile grew coy. Their ride continued a good magical amount of time further.

*

At one point Yan noticed the silhouette of a building rise above everything else, above where he knew the riverbank was. As the cab approached, they could hardly see the top of it through the persistent curtains of mist waving up from the streetlamps, ever upwards unto where the high-rise vanished into the pitch sky. Out from that vault of night, one of its magnificent facades cascaded in robust curves like a Romanesque fountain frozen in concrete, frozen in time. The structure cast its imperceptible shadow over the two youth upon the sidewalk where the driver had dropped them off. Fah pulled Yan down the block to the building's front. A startled old stray dog growled at them ineffectually from beyond the meager gates blocking their entry.

"I hope you're at peace with your spirits," she said oddly as they paused, both somewhat in awe at the massive abandoned edifice.

Bangkok was a veritable graveyard-full of these slumbering giants, empty towering skeletons ever since the economic crash of '97. But that was before these two were born, and these many architectural tombs were really nothing more than familiar landmarks on the city map anymore, right? They couldn't possibly be haunted. No one's ever had the opportunity to live inside them. And while Fah and Yan both knew that grownups tell stories only to keep kids from risking the very real dangers that lie inside, deep in their hearts they separately feared that this unfinished hotel might nevertheless be home to ghosts.

"How did you find out about this place?"

"My uncle's company was about to help clean up this wreck. I nabbed the blueprints from his files," Fah bragged.

Aged vines strangled the dormant monster's arches and columns. Two escalators ascending to nowhere marked the front. Fah took Yan by the hand and showed him a hidden climb to the threshold of the lobby.

Imagine the fear that suffocated Yan's heart when he understood the totality of darkness through which they were to travel. His vision was instantaneously eclipsed. He instinctively clenched Fah's hand tightly, feeling suddenly powerless to even move. He severely doubted the reckless pace his guide was setting. The human body is so frail, he thought to himself.

"I trust you know where you're going? I mean, I wouldn't want to have to blame you for falling fifty floors to my death."

"Why would you do a thing like that. Trust me, I mean?" He didn't find her jokes at all assuring. "Now try to be quiet, at least for a bit. I want to make sure no one else is in here," she heightened Yan's mounting apprehension with.

Every step she dragged him onward, Yan felt tentatively with his tiptoe first, so as to be certain he wasn't about to plant his entire weight into a gaping hole. At the top of every staircase, he mistakenly overstepped the landing in anticipation of one more stair. He was completely disoriented. The only occasional illumination were thin glimpses of the city lights that seemed to dance before one's blotted eyes like spectral wisps. Sounds from the streets below echoed around the interior and confused the already helpless senses. Yan lost perspective as to his body's relationship with its surroundings and at one point felt like he knew what it was like to be a spirit trapped inside a spirit house. Occasionally a draft through the paneless windows would wet his cheek like a chill phantom touch. Though he recognized the shape and thinness of Fah's fingers in his hand, Yan began to wonder if it wasn't perhaps instead some stranger's, some cunning demon's that was leading him headlong toward a horrible end. What choice did he have but to follow?

"Fah? Fah, can you please say something?"

"Will you please keep quiet, you big baby? We'll be there soon..."

Just then a steely bang came echoing from the floors above. Followed by another.

"It's just old pipes," Fah insisted unconvincingly.

"Crap, there's some-...someone else in here!" Yan stammered.

"Shut up, damn it!"

Yan obeyed, but his chin wouldn't stop trembling. He felt like he could hear his heart beat throughout the invisible space of the room in which they were now hopelessly frozen. Was it his own pulse or Fah's that pounded in their desperate grasp?

Three quick strikes came ringing over their heads, so much closer now. Something dire, something angry in that sharp rhythm. For but an instant Yan thought he saw, in the darkest of blindness, a black figure descending a stairway down upon his very head. He instinctively crumpled to the ground. His fear had betrayed him—he'd let go Fah's hand.

Chapter 15: Somewhere Altogether Different

This particular cat showed no sign of fear. Mr Torpong had always had an affinity for domesticated animals, an extensive category by his own calculations, having grown up on a farm nestled at the feet of the wild mountains of the north. Throughout his rural upbringing he had in turn caught and tamed as pets a tree frog, a beetle, a starling, a forest rooster and a snake. But never once a cat, though he'd often wished for one. He bent down to scratch behind her ears. There was a certain kindling in the animal's pupils, a distinct spark of soul. Kneeling to the feline, Torpong blocked out the city sounds and lights about him and floated a while longer on the waves of childhood memories lapping over him.

"I think I'll call you Boonnam. You're my lucky find," he sweetly muttered.

Oddly, since moving to the city, he'd never bothered to get another pet, though he did often stop to greet the occasional amicable alley dog or cat. This straggler had recently given birth. In truth she looked seasoned enough to have pushed out a half-dozen litters upon the streets. Torpong pitied all these abandoned animals, perhaps for their being trapped here inside this nature-starved city. Somewhere, this little tender mother must have had a home with her kittens somewhere. Suddenly the cat moved from his reach and departed abruptly yet demurely. He followed without question.

Boonnam, as she was now called, straightaway exited the noisy roundabout eastward beneath the Skytrain. Mr Torpong was surprised at the animal's determination as he watched her swollen teats swing with each step. The two continued down to Santiphap Park, where the animal eventually relaxed her pace in order to explore various shrubs along its outskirts.

Torpong tried to keep track of her from outside the park's gate as she wistfully wove between the railings. Sometimes he lost sight of her and felt embarrassed loitering whenever people passed. Had he lost her to the trees for good? But then she returned to sight at the corner. Both promptly took right back to the sidewalk, the one in front, the other behind.

From here on out the city offered less lush distraction and their journey progressed more resolutely. The two turned southeastward, down and even across some pretty hectic boulevards.

No matter, for Boonnam was the ever-expert guide, never once endangering her willing charge. All Mr Torpong knew was that he was compelled to follow, for the cat's sake, because the cat had chosen to lead. The further they progressed, the more he felt he knew the location where they were going, though he also knew it wasn't so much a place they sought. And it was with this unique sort of empathetic conviction that the duration and distance of their unwavering pilgrimage dissolved into meaning-lessness as readily as the daytime hours do into the depths of night.

Chapter 16: Eurydice Triumphant

"This is what you want me to smoke? After that fright?" Fah held up a pack of condoms before her face, laughing. You could just make out her pigtails lashing against the nighttime sky. "You nabbed *these* from the store?" Yan was relieved she couldn't make out his embarrassment in the dark. At last her chuckling stopped and the two silently scanned the cityscape from their spot upon the balcony. The gentle breeze was warm, yet Fah clung to his arm more tightly and he could feel her still trembling despite her mirth.

The mist had ceased and small dim patches of stars began to peek through the clouds opening overhead. Below was Wat Yannawa, whose chofah glinted weakly from the depths. In the distance Yan could see the wide black swath of the Chao Phraya cut through the mosaic of city lights. The chant-like churning of boats up and down its breadth floated to their ears muffled by the erratic roadway traffic. Yan's still mixed-up state of fear and humiliation slowly eased while he observed the tiny motorbikes and cars traversing Taksin Bridge. Those two endless streams of lights, sometimes single, sometimes paired, in either direction across the river, like flocks in oppositional migration. The transmigration of souls across the opaque waters.

"We must be a thousand meters high. I feel like I'm in the clouds," Yan sighed.

"I hate to disappoint you, sugar. We're only twelve floors up. Hardly a quarter the way."

"Well, still, it's the highest I've ever..." he tried to blunt her slight as he glanced up and around at the black mass towering over.

The fact of the matter was he knew Fah wasn't mentioning how, during that moment they'd lost touch, she'd heard him cry out like a baby. That was how he'd felt back there alone and blind. Somewhere deep in his brain, Yan could still hear the echoing clangs. But Fah had found him in a flash, though it seemed it took near an eternity. And the clanging never returned. And she had somehow safely guided them to this amazing gallery upon the city.

He was unsure whether it was the energy of the city spreading before them, or if it was because they'd found a momentary sanctuary above, but in a strange way now he felt his salvation not only bound to Fah, but also to the paths of Bangkok's multitude of souls below.

Yan tried to fix upon her eyes in the shadows that played across her cheeks, which seemed to shed a glow of their own into the shrouding night. The stars began to spread wide around her profile. At last the full moon brewed from behind the thinning wisps, bathing both the building and Fah in a similar hue. How beautiful is woman's body, Yan thought, and when he saw her turn and raise her face to his: "There are times when I think I shall be forgotten by you."

She vexed him with her quiet. Yan could only interpret a sliver of what that silence meant. For behind her affectations of sorrow or bliss at whatever else Yan thought to confess during the remainder of that night, Fah perfectly concealed the fact that she'd seen something of her own back there, when she'd been in that utter blackness of the building's deep interior by herself.

Chapter 17: Something Altogether Different

Boonnam climbed up the stairs and straightaway to the ankles of the boy looking over the side of the bridge. It was the same canal Mr Torpong peered heavenward from the very night before, the one he'd revisited just that afternoon. But tonight Torpong dared not exceed the stairway's shadows from where he could watch unnoticed. The lone boy knelt down to meet the cat in much the same manner he himself had about an hour ago. What was a kid his age doing out so late? Apparently our little Boonnam got around.

You could've almost overlooked the two, the cat and the boy, so immersed they were in their private greeting. But once you'd spotted them, you couldn't help but drink in the ripening emotion, however understated it might have looked at first. For each appeared to recognize a sworn friend in the other, two friends seeking refuge in the other's warmth. Or perhaps it was that Boonnam seemed to react to a certain gravity in the boy, which Torpong thought he himself had in some degree sensed.

It's difficult to say what exactly conveyed this, this joy tinged with care, whether it was how the boy lilted his small curled back in submission, or his absent-minded petting. Or maybe it was something inherent to the quiet of the hour instead, the lapping waters of the canal distinctly heard. The scene's solemnness proved as elusive yet unmistakable as the tone of a landscape in the hands of a watercolorist eulogizing the impermanence of the world's beauty. Torpong began to feel guilty for desecrating the moment, and yet he watched, attempting to peer through to some deeper meaning. It was a bit of a relief, like that after a long meditation, when the boy got up from the cat, turned his glance down to the canal a brief and final time, then descended the north side. The cat remained where the boy had left her.

Torpong stuck his head over the edge the moment he reached the top, the cat brushing his ankle. Upon the waters he noticed a vague shadow extending from that cast by the bridge, shifting with the waves next to his own head's faint shadow. He sprung his head around with a start, fearing someone had suddenly snuck up behind. But there were only the buildings and streetlights, a lone motorbike. He looked over the edge again, studying the strange watery shadow still expanding into his. He glanced over his shoulder again, just to make certain. Where had the cat gone off to? Then down to the churning, calling waters, the stone-like city and the depthless sky above effortlessly transformed into exponential splits and shifts of light and black below.

Were those crumpled scraps of paper, or were those silhouettes of flowers in that liquid play of colors, bobbing further and further apart from each other? Trembling in rhythmic succession, ripple upon ripple. Off into the fatal unseen tide alone.

Chapter 18: The Dream

It's a wonder that rest ever did come to Mr Torpong, so rampant were his thoughts on that solitary journey back to his apartment. His brain flashed feverishly the whole way, bitter almost at the impenetrability of what he'd seen, what he'd undergone. Even if it'd all meant nothing, which his rational part kept insisting to itself, there nonetheless remained that sorrow, that inexplicable sense of loss that had pierced him through atop that bridge. As often as the image of those flowers disappearing into the shadows returned to mind, Torpong's throat clenched and tears began to heat along his trembling lids. And by the time his feet had trudged him dumbly through the long route home, a hypnotic depression had so overcome his heart with its potions, he had no choice but to succumb to sleep. His body sank at last into its bed as if into an oozing underwater mud.

He dreamt he was wandering the city in the hour just before dawn. He dreamt he was going from tree to tree, gathering fruit. But instead of fruit, it was people hanging from the branches. Their bodies were limp and weighty when he first grabbed them by their shirt collars, by their belts or shoelaces to pluck them free, but then became malleable, like fading ghosts in his arms which kept them in their eternal slumber with a soothing rocking. Their closed lids were dry and smooth and frail, like the outer shell of langsat. When he peeled back the flecked tawny coating, inside he found the milky flesh of the fruit, so ripe you could almost taste its tartness. Then Torpong would softly stuff one of these spirits, and then another into his bottomless jacket pocket. The still ungathered shadows filled the yellowish fog that crept along the streets. Some hung so far above his head amid the ancient trees, he had to stretch to heights that made him dizzy. He was constantly wiping away mist that pooled his eyelashes and grew anxious at the thought he'd have to continue without the use of sight. How long must he labor thus, forgetting thousands upon thousands of insubstantial corpses' faces, racing to finish the harvest before the sun came? What if there were some that simply remained out of reach?

Chapter 19: His Mother Was Going to Kill Him

Nothing hung suspended from the young boy's neck—of this Yan was astutely aware. Night was only now growing pale again, as it had been at its birth some twelve hours ago. He needed to get home to change into his school uniform. What if he didn't make it back before his mother awoke? Just how long had he been without his amulet?

If Fah had slipped it from him without mention, Yan had to admit the signs of her kleptomania were there all along for him to see. Yan began to fear he didn't even know the most prudent path home. The concrete slabs seemed to crack, to jut and to tilt beneath each of his hurried steps.

Have you ever noticed some obstacle before you in the road, some hazard you knew you'd need to circum-navigate? And you probably said to yourself, "I foresee I'm going to trip on that broom-handle" or "That dog is going to nip my ankle." And sure enough, despite any potential benefit in the premonition, that is precisely what happens, however trivial the outcome.

Well Yan began to have this tangible and mildly irritating sense of something about to happen, except without the gratification of a visible threat. Rather it was more a precise point in space, just there about thirty meters off to the side, halfway across the road at the base of a Skytrain pillar. Yan felt in the pit of his stomach that at the same moment he would release his breath, that point in the corner of his vision was going to explode with an unworldly cry.

And still the car rolled right on by, slowly and unpresumptuous into the bottomless timeframe of a single human breath, its axle nearly silently snapping and the one front tire gently peeling off and rolling into some bushes. That almost song-like shriek, that squeal, boom and glassy downpour alone thundered the sinister demon's entrance—of death's entrance—of what surely was another human's death!

Not the subsequently surreal vision of the automobile wrecked upon the chipped concrete support; nor the disparate cries from windows and doorways, and gesticulating bodies conglomerating, barely woken from sleep; not the unanswerable questions, the unsure commands; nothing that followed. Not the distant shout of: "...dead...the lady's dead, okay..."; not the sporadic honking of a passing motorbike, the eventual crescendo of sirens from what must be every city corner, nothing else that happened after could herald it. Only that first fatal scream still rang it loudly, rang out that ravenous Chance was right at heel, the impossible now made deadly whole. Chance cares not who it crushes, so long as it keeps rolling.

Paralyzed, Yan could only watch the scene unfold like a performance he'd not been meant to see. In the actors' rhythmic motions around the crash, he only saw the fiery spinning spokes of Chance, its muddied wheels rumbling onward until it crushes the full of every monsoon's briefly blossoming weeds. Stubborn and indifferent, because Chance knows it has more than time enough to finally crush them all.

From out of the growing, dancing crowd, a police official stepped back and looked unconcernedly away from it all, from where everyone else was transfixed, and dead at Yan instead.

Chapter 20: An Official Query

Mr Torpong didn't know how to react at first when he saw the small white envelope with the royal seal left on the middle of his desk. The fact that it bore no single form of address is what made it stand out so. Torpong scanned the always empty office before reaching down to open it:

What do you know about the child who drowned?

Nothing more. Phrased as an anonymous question, yes. But more of an unquestionable accusation.

Chapter 21: A Subtler Shade of Pink

It's instructive how different the world can be when you wake earlier than the thirty minutes required to brush your hair, put on makeup, tweak the school skirt and scurry off to class, though it was no newly resolved self-discipline that tore Pink from her cherished sleep at such an ungodly hour lately. Rather it was the dreams for nearly the past week. As she lay there in the dark of her room, still shaken from this latest nightmare, trying to piece the scant fragments left to her, she realized that a vague anxiety for her little cousin was at the heart of her troubled nights. Or perhaps a kind of fear.

Would the sun never appear? She had no use for this endless turning in one's sheets.

Pink rose and undertook a quiet reenactment of her morning ritual. The whole rest of the house still slept when she finally popped closed the front door behind.

Outside the chatter of birds in the branches seemed to draw forth the first colors of the day. The mutter of sporadic traffic bubbled further and further up into the weave of chirping overhead. The previous night's rain must have summoned every worm from every crack and crevice, for the birds' it sounded like an eager song.

The transience of the moment, the delicate hue of this short-lived transition between the tranquility of night and the barely envisioned coming day, it spellbound Pink, who must have forgotten such fairytale pictures could still exist. But even now, when Pink was long done with fairytales, Bangkok offered up such delectable mysteries. And Pink thought to herself that there is nothing so at once sad and joyful as the fated dying of the night, day after day after day.

Here is when she saw a furtive shadow on the opposite side of the street skirting from trunk to tree trunk. Some tardy ghost retiring from its nightly haunt. The swagger and the pigtails exposed it all—it was Fah!

"Where the fuck are you going? What've you got Yan up to this time?" Pink raspily hurled past the motorbike sputtering up the road between them. Fah stopped and looked her way, scrutinizing for a moment the distant voice. It took but a heartbeat for her to identify the pink hair gleaming brightly in the dawn and to march across the street straight up to her accuser. When those belligerent pigtails were aimed right into Pink's contorting face, this was all the younger spoke.

"You don't even know him, do you? You don't even know your own cousin," Fah defied.

"Who the hell—?"

"There's something you couldn't guess! That he himself can't know!" Then she briskly turned and skittered off across the way, back from the direction she'd come, like some petulant bird.

Chapter 22: Mongkut on the Job

Here are the indisputable facts Royal Thai Police Sergeant Mongkut was able to uncover concerning the boy who'd drowned:

1. The body was found by a friend that morning floating in San Saep Canal;
2. The boy, who'd flunked several courses, had gone to school in Petchburi district and had lived nearby on soi 31;
3. The boy's father owned a seafood restaurant in the same neighborhood;
4. Conveniently, his mother worked as a clerk for the city's Health Inspection Department;
5. His family was already grieving over the recent loss of the boy's elder sister, a known suicide;
6. Contrary to the position of official police documents, there was no material evidence to substantiate the boy was also a suicide.

The reader can probably distinguish between those which he gathered in a neat list left behind on his desk for all the world to see, and those which, come the end of the workday, he exited the department's front doors with, locked away in his brain.

As the sergeant descended the front steps unto the boulevard cooling in the evening air, bowing and smiling amiably to the locals along his way who knew him and his honorable name quite well, his thoughts began to turn to the modest but familiar comforts of his home, where he'd lived since childhood until long after both parents had died. The prospect of finishing the scant household chores and at last crawling into bed with nothing to come between him and the pages of a good book helped to enliven his step.

Chapter 23: A Lovers' Game

Maybe it was the lingering menace of the car crash he'd watched, or the delirium from having been up all night, but Yan felt desperate to be back together with Fah. Nothing short could quell the ache inside his heart. He didn't know how he'd possibly stay awake until the two of them could lie arm in arm again, in the grass, and he could tell her what he'd seen, and maybe nap on her lap before class. At least until some outraged teacher arrived upon the scene unfolding in Yan's imagination.

However come that reunion, it was apparent Fah had concocted altogether different plans. Grander plans to be exact, specifically in the number of invited. Who was this overgrown pest of a third-wheel, elbows propped arrogantly against the gate, uncomfortably close to Yan's lover? Yan had never seen him before, not even in the upper grades.

"I'm Yan," he introduced himself with tepid confidence. "You must be new here too," he nodded, indicating Fah.

"Are you high, sugar? Just who you trying to prank!" Fah's scolding startled him. He hadn't expected resistance from this direction.

"I know, listen to your songbird's adorable twittering," the other joined right in. Where did this son-of-a-bitch, with his flipped-up collar, sculpted hair and thousand-baht sneakers, get off calling him Fah's pet?

"Well okay then Yan, let me be the first to introduce you to my big cousin," Fah announced in a ridiculously formal tone, "This here is the honorable Somchai. You know, whose house I'm living in for the year." Then turning to the other, "Somchai, this is my boyfriend, Yan. My forgetful cuckoo."

Yan found his position in this absurd triangle acutely diminishing. He couldn't conceive what sort of wicked joke Fah was being so quick to join in.

" He is...he's just like a little bird," Somchai piled on. "Unless he's right there chirping at you, you forget he's even there."

"Now ease up." And here Fah did finally put her arm around Yan somewhat consolingly. "You'll learn to love the soul inside the same way I do." Yan was already fuming too hotly for her half-hearted retraction to register at all.

So then, this was the way things now worked. Not only could the heavens nullify the existence of a best friend, not only could they in a heartbeat enthrall you in a wild romance, but now it seemed this upheaved universe could conjure any annoying variety of blood-relation from out of thin air. Still, had the workings of this earth really changed the least? Was this latest inexplicable triviality any more meaningless than the horrific crash he'd witnessed but an hour back? The more Yan thought it through, attempting to block out Fah and Somchai's ongoing slights, the more it terrified him how the thunderous phenomenon of beholding another's death had somehow evolved into this ludicrousness of these two fools blathering on and on.

All he wanted was to be alone.

He could imagine how Toi would've teased him on this particular occasion: "It's not the other boys you should worry about; it's your future brother-in-law."

It's understandable why Yan decided to zip his lip from here on out. He wished he'd zipped it the night before. He began to wonder if the silence didn't suit him better.

Chapter 24: Where There's Not Smoke

"My sincerest apologies, Sergeant, but we are not presently in possession of the body," the medical examiner informed Mongkut matter-of-factly. The morgue almost arithmetically reflected the tidiness of the examiner's words. Mongkut had to at least commend him here on this: on a thorough tidiness. Indeed this was precisely the reason he plainly hated coming down. The room was completely devoid of what Mongkut could only describe as due and proper ceremony. Sure, there was a necessary order, near absolute in fact. The linens neatly folded and awaiting use inside the glass-doored cabinets; the waist bins freshly emptied. But the sergeant found himself focusing instead on the corpses still left out, apparently unfinished with yet, and he tried to imagine the intricacies of their past lives. Was that thin arm exposed over there, sticking out from the shadows, the arm of a woman? Dead as that woman in the car this morning. What had been the events that had brought this one here, of all possible places and outcomes? Now for these poor souls, all sensations and memories and thoughts of the bodily had ceased. The dead, they had nothing else to give, nothing left to bequeath except for maybe their concluded stories, the dwindling ripples of their influence onto this living and forgetful world. And then there were the ones in the bags for good. It creeped the hell out of Mongkut.

How many cadavers had this young man in the spotless lab-coat seen before he'd stopped thinking about the spirits that once inhabited them? The examiner blinked at the sergeant emptily from behind his perfectly round glasses. How many thousands of emptied eyes would stare into that one indifferent pair as their last before cremation? A million souls could pass into the beyond through the tidy span of those glimmering sister glass circles.

"Here's the record of the body being released. But I can't locate the paperwork for the corpse's arrival," the examiner offered after some pause. "Would you like to see the one parent's signature?" Monkgut found the qualification of quantity strange.

"No, but I thank you, sir. I do not think there will be any further need right now of your most honorable services."

Chapter 25: The Gage is Down

Fah probably hadn't meant much harm by it, but Yan's feelings were injured nonetheless. Not one of the insults she and Somchai had volleyed, with Yan's silent spectatorship almost central to their sport, none of it rang the slightest bit true, did it? Was he really anything like a pesky bird? After all, Yan knew who he was; he was the best positioned judge. Hadn't he been there his whole life?

Even those faults he'd never willingly confess, he still could acknowledge them internally, or at times at least subconsciously, like a fruit caught in the corner of the eye day after day, ripening neglected upon your kitchen table. A handful of expected things could happen to such a fruit, a mangosteen let's say: the flies might get it; it may end up on the family alter; a boy grab and eat it. But along any of those life's stages, would the passerby ever dare to confront the thing and defiantly declare: "No. You are no longer a fruit. You are a mere seed. No, the supple parent flower still. Now just a bud. Now only the light from the sun before it kisses the divine pollen." And will the silently awaiting thing obey? It will continue rather to age and rot. Can one undo what has been done?

"Girl trouble, Yan?" Master Nagani greeted him condescendingly at the doorway. Was this going to become a daily interrogation? The man really was evil incarnate. Yan was beginning to wish he'd never painted the professor in such a ridiculously sinister light, for now it seemed he'd be the one who was going to pay for it. At the back of the line of students filing in, he took his seat without replying to the question.

It was though with a sudden unease that he noticed the altered arrangement of the room: there was Toi's empty desk directly across. Just yesterday…it had been missing yesterday, right? It could only have returned to serve as a private reminder, like a bare stone to mark a grave that meant nothing to anybody else. To gaze upon daily from here on out.

"And now, students, it's time for roll," the professor commenced.

A name and nothing more, whose one true iteration Yan would never speak again…

"Petch?"

"Here, master," Petch answered.

"Pim?"

"Here, master," Pim answered.

Toi, how did you escape this ludicrous hell? Who was having the last laugh now? And though it felt presumptuous guessing what his dead friend would think, Yan couldn't help a smirk as he entertained the many things Toi might have said.

"Somchai? Somchai! Oh there. Now why is it you're late...*again*?"

"I was talking with a girl of course," Somchai announced with all the sarcasm he could muster. The class blurted out a nearly unanimous laugh.

"Perhaps then it might please you to explain why you couldn't show up to even one minute of class yesterday, boy," Nagani held the line once quiet had resumed.

"Oh sure, I was here. Maybe you just forgot to call my name."

No one was laughing now. Especially not Master Nagani.

Then with a sort of melodramatic disdain, Somchai took the desk that had been Toi's.

Chapter 26: The Hot Seat

Mr Torpong wasn't sure how to proceed with the rest of his day now that he'd read the letter, so he decided it best to do exactly as he had every workday prior: hanging up his jacket, warming up the computer, steeping a pot of tea, straightening the papers he'd carried up with him earlier that morning right before he'd found the note. This time though the ritual was carried out with an unfamiliar anxiety. He caught himself slouching motionless in his seat, staring at his reflection in the screen for unknown minutes. What had taken hold of him? What was it about the office that had suddenly become so foreboding? Surely it was the message in the letter, so bare yet so laden. Then was it a sneaking guilt he was suffering? A guilt which Torpong knew he was spotlessly innocent of. Or perhaps it was because of the boy he'd seen last night. No—it must be another! It couldn't be the same child as in the letter. But the notion had already taken seat in his heart and Mr Torpong noticed in his reflection upon the greenish screen something like a tear trickling down his cheek beneath his glasses.

Then came the knock at the door.

Torpong spun in his chair, uncertain what to do. The one thing he did know was that, whoever was on the other side, whatever errand that stranger was on, it had nothing to do with Torpong's normal routine as it had stood up until this morning.

When he pulled the jiggling knob, how relieved he was to discover it was a her...I mean it was a woman. She smiled so sweetly throughout her mannered bow. Her hair was pulled back tightly in a bun, the pearls hanging from either ear small and simple, old-fashioned. Her face was bright and inviting. It was difficult to penetrate that face's age, to surmise the source of its beauty—whether it was a spark of youth, or experience's grace. Was hers not unlike the face of a remembered lover? Might she not easily have also been somebody's mother?

"Good day, Mr Torpong. I've been told to see you," the woman's smile grew to reveal two rows of perfectly nacreous teeth.

"Good day to you too. Yes, okay, thank you for asking. And for you...?" Torpong trailed off, anticipating an introduction.

"I will leave you my card after the meeting," outmaneuvering his awkward cue. "We have business to attend to first." With a diffident nod in return, Torpong pretended to comprehend.

So, theirs was to be a meeting of some sort. It must be a royal governmental matter she was alluding to, which the envelope's official seal supported. But why again Torpong? Frankly she was beginning to frighten him with her dizzying mix of congeniality, imperiousness and sheer elusiveness. She walked directly to Torpong's desk, slapped her briefcase upright onto it, turned and brushed his chair cushion three times, sat down, and swiveled back around to look him in the eyes. He didn't know how to react to this invasion of his workplace.

"Please expand on what you know," her smile narrowed.

Why had she used *expand*? Had he already admitted to something? Mr Torpong tasted a rancid swill pool in his throat as he tried to swallow. He thought his face must look very ugly to this beautiful and stately woman. He felt like a schoolboy that had just been asked a question he hadn't studied for. He really did wish he knew the answer. If only he might be allowed his office back to himself, then he might be able to think this whole thing through and maybe come up with something and get back to her. Her knitting brow conveyed a mounting impatience with the prolonged silence.

"Do I need to repeat the question," she graciously offered.

Thirty-one. For some absurd reason, the words *thirty-one* kept popping into his head. But he couldn't answer her that.

"No."

"You know, there are just two types in this world. Just two. I've only ever had to deal with two kinds of men." Whatever she really meant, things were becoming squarely inappropriate. "Which are you?" The woman spun back around and snatched her briefcase from the desk, knocking off a folder. She kept her face from him thereafter, as if to assure she was completely finished with the pathetic Mr Torpong.

She also neglected to leave her card. Torpong reached to rub his eyes beneath his glasses and realized he'd never wiped the trickle of tear away. What a fool. At least he had his office to himself again.

Chapter 27: He Had To

He had to find the boy, the one still alive who'd found his friend dead in the water. There was obviously more to the story of the drowning than could fit on any police report. Where better to start than with the friend himself?

Afternoon's heat was mellowing in Ratchthewi when the sergeant stepped off the train and down the staircase to the street below. It was but a short and pleasant stroll to the neighborhoods just north of Chitlom station. School had long since let out and it was with a sort of irresistible nostalgia that, along his way, Mongkut watched the sporadic clusters of playful children capitalizing on the sun's last rays. Their thousand kinds of games and laughter was a profound delight.

The whole of Petchburi provides so much more that's edifying than could ever be salvaged from the murkier city depths his line of work tended to drag him. Here instead, despite the neighborhood's energy and momentum, all is at peace with the world. Workers feel the day's weariness fall from their shoulders as quick as they lock the office up behind. Night shops illuminate their modest signs. Fishy aromas float from the restaurants to whet the appetites of those gathering outside. Bosses text other bosses while waiting for the street attendant to move the street blockade out of the way. *The night is still so young!* That sentiment seemed at the corners of every passing smile.

Mongkut too was glad to be outdoors. He bought a paper at the corner stall...soi 35...he winked at a group of giggling girls passing by...soi 34...now what on earth could that tumult be he heard brewing up ahead? When the sergeant turned the corner, he encountered an alarming scene.

A group of boys closed in around a single boy, who was blindfolded and clinging to a broomstick for some reason. The child was sorely outnumbered. One of his tormentors in particular, a tall kid yanking the other end of the stick, rallied the throng of punks clambering right up on the one pinned in the middle. Mongkut jumped to and repelled the cowards away with a flurry of thumps from his paper about their ears and shouts of "chicken-shit no-goods!" The big kid was the last intent on doing some damage, but jerking the broomstick free, he too at last relented, swirling the trophy over his head as he scurried around the corner.

The sergeant brushed off the back of the child on the ground and checked for injuries even before helping remove the handkerchief. He looked so pathetic crumpled over with his head tucked into his arms: it softened Mongkut's heart. He slowly lifted and turned the boy, cradling his torso in the tuck of his arm so as to reassure and examine his front. Though the boy's pants were torn, there was nothing serious beyond a scraped knee and a split lip.

"It's okay. You're not alone anymore," the sergeant said, rolling the blindfold over the back of his head. "They're gone. What happened?"

"Nothing. Just a game," the boy deflected, his voice still trembling in heaves from the strain of fear.

"Some game! Nothing but the losing end for you," Mongkut joked, regretting it as soon as he'd said it. "Hold still now, I've nearly got this knot."

When he removed the handkerchief, Mongkut noticed tears in the child's eyes. When he opened them to behold his protector, the boy appeared even more terrified. The sergeant realized he'd seen him before. Something in that face's roundness. Him, it had been him at that car crash this morning. Mongkut recalled it clearly: how the boy had caught his attention, staring at the horrible aftermath of the accident as if hypnotized. Hadn't their glances met this morning too, in what now seemed a vanished flash a lifetime apart? Perhaps the child didn't recognize him without his uniform.

"Did you hear the voice too? Did you see her?" the youth demanded. The question appeared to pain him further.

"I don't know if...only the other kid who..." Mongkut stumbled, unsure of what he was fishing for. "Do you live around here? We should get you home to your parents."

But the boy didn't answer. Sitting up on his own, he looked aslant for a spell so he didn't have to endure the sergeant's prying gaze. Mongkut allowed him a moment to get his bearings back. The child at last rose, wiped his nose with his arm, careful of the lip, and walked away without saying another word. Mongkut thought it duly respectful to stay and watch the tiny battered specter resign himself into the shadows.

The sergeant decided to try and track down the instigator of the assault instead. But when he turned into the alley by which the culprit had escaped, he bumped into a girl crouching right around the corner. She got back to her feet clumsily and stared up at him defiantly, sticking her tongue out between two fingers at him. Maybe if he flashed his badge, this pigtailed brat might learn some manners!

Chapter 28: Payback in Pink

It was only a matter of time before Pink found out what'd happened. Fuck that useless piece of shit Somchai! She was going to kill him *and* his traitorous cousin! Everyone was whispering about how Fah had been secretly egging Somchai on from the sidelines the whole damn time. Poor Yan. How was he going to survive? Pink even heard some crazy guy showed up and broke things up.

Oh world beware the consummation of a big cousin's rage and cunning! How savory the myriad ways one might proceed; how many terrible denouements she might devise! Which might be the cruelest, the tastiest? No doubt history's greatest schemers thought on their feet throughout each sinister tiptoe up unto the final scene. Pink had to make certain Yan didn't catch wind, or else she'd be sure to lose him to Fah for good. She also understood she ought to try and console her little cousin but had no clear idea how to go about it.

As Pink climbed the stairway to her bedroom, dialing the roughly hundred digits of her closest confidants, it was precisely that. It was neglecting matters that mattered most that may have been her initial misstep.

Chapter 29: A Sudden Loss of Appetite

A fat lip will remind you of its pain every time you try to speak. That injury though was not the reason Yan kept silent the whole way home. For once in his life he felt relieved his mother wouldn't be there. Finding the kitchen table unusually bare in truth brought no additional pang or sorrow. Yan wasn't hungry in the least.

Even if he had just imagined Fah laughing in the background, he knew, he plainly sensed she'd been there master-minding the cruel attack. With each subsequent blow he'd blindly tried to block, Yan had only been able to think the one recurring plea: "Why did you abandon me without my amulet?" Long after the brutes and she had fled, the question expanded into widening rings of meaning with each reiteration. That crazy interfering man, he should've just let them finish the job.

Yan soaked a dark rag in the sink and put it to the split in his lower lip. The cloth absorbed a sizeable blot. He tried to examine the wound in his reflection in the kitchen window. The squinting face there returning his glance, who was that person? Its identity seemed strange and unknowable. Could this possibly be the face that he'd become? It looked older than the memories Yan felt able to summon. The eyes, so bright and round once, glaring now with an unwavering scorn he never dreamt he'd taste. The longer he peered into his own image, the more he understood precisely who it was that visage in the glass was mocking and hated.

At least he was alone, safe and by himself.

Long ago, before he'd met Toi, Yan had considered himself alone. And though this loneliness brought great anxiety at the time, he now saw how this long lost self-reliance had also been unappreciatedly pure and tranquil. True peace, but gone. For then of course Toi came along, a mere ghost anymore, but still a nagging ghost. And then Fah. Yan had no way anymore to claim himself alone. That recollected self, hardly recognizable behind the one he examined in the glass, was as unreachable as if that child had never existed. With this sort of self-dissection, the meaning of the image in the pane slowly began to submerge beneath its own sorrow.

Yan and his reflection peered beyond one another, down to the streets below, down to the city: the hurtling cars and motorbikes; the endless streams of strangers up and down, some to eat and some to pray, some to sin and some to sleep; the trees and shrubs that meditatively steeped in the exhaust and heat. It too—the immortal city—if it could hold a heavenly mirror to its own face, would the city also marvel at its manifold but steady change? And if you ripped away the mask it'd shaped generation after generation—nothing but the black primordial river that pumps and cleaves its age-maddened heart!

Yan looked back to the blood on the rag, his own blood, darkening the rag even more. There was no escape back into that craved for solitude: he was enveloped by too many others. He had committed himself unto too many. How to deny that multitude of damning voices? The one that rang most shrilly was the memory of Fah's treacherous laugh.

When he was sure the bleeding had stopped, he rinsed the towel as clean as he could so that his mother wouldn't notice. Then he went to his room and undressed, stuffing his stained, torn clothes to the pit of the laundry, where they could hide until he washed them.

As Yan then lay in bed in the dark, listening to the sounds of the city, he dwelled for some while, and with some relief no less, upon how there remained the one immutable path to absolute solitude left open to this world...open and forever awaiting all who fill this world. And he wondered if he'd ultimately made an unholy oath in embracing it.

So simply did he find his way to sleep that night without the need to weep.

Chapter 30: How Do These Things Begin?

For no sound reason, and despite a good lack of sleep, Mr Torpong enjoyed an unusually chipper morning next morning. A youthful excitement quickened his step across the sidewalk slabs and intersecting boulevards in anticipation of finally savoring the air his office promised. There was no explaining either his mood or how one's place of work might attain a certain atmosphere after the visit of a woman. But sure enough her initial smile, whatever its real intent, had bewitched him through and through.

Torpong just stood there in the middle of his office for a while studying the scant traces of her bodily presence: the unusual position of the chair, the folder still littering the floor. With some conscious effort he'd left it all untouched the day before. The mysterious letter however was mysteriously missing. When it'd gone, no one could say. For Mr Torpong had in truth essentially blocked out all the circumstances surrounding this element. That message and its forgotten portent had all but flown from memory as swift as the angel imprinted on it. Instead he reflected back to how he'd spent most last night rolling awake in bed puzzling over the woman's parting challenge: *which will you be?* What exactly did the question hope to inspire? Or had he been the butt of some bizarre joke?

Though he could admit to a palpably pleasant tingle in his bum when he first took his chair, after a time there was no excuse to not get to straightening up.

It's a shame how mundane tasks overtake what once seemed most important. Soon enough had Torpong reestablished the familiarly disheveled piles of paper on his desk. He'd squirmed in and squeaked his chair so often by late morning, he couldn't recall how she'd abruptly left it anymore. The letters and numbers rippling across his computer screen danced about his eyeballs without meaning. Whenever he glanced over his shoulder at the door, he could only picture it as it remained: unpromisingly closed. When he finally went to cheer himself with some tea, he discovered he'd already finished his cup.

He watched the shape of the light through his window modulate across the floor and began to realize it was this selfsame workplace routine that was eroding his memory of the woman. If he didn't do something soon, he'd lose all recollection of that maddening smile. Then where'd he be? The same place he was yesterday before the knock upon that door. He consulted his wristwatch one last time. In another fifteen minutes he'd have no choice but to leave. Must he never hear her voice again? How could he possibly go home now, to only come back and endure another day like today? Evening though was winning out.

There comes a point when you have to confess opportunity is all but lost. The sooner you relinquish false hope, the sooner you can get back to and keep your head above the daily ripples. The population of the city can all too readily ignore the lone pedestrian submerged in such depressing thoughts. Bangkok's million frenetic winds cannot sustain such concentrated weight. Thus will the whip-and-whirl of city life howl yet rebound and only serve to sink him further. And with an invisible stealth did an unsolvable knot of introspection now envelope Torpong like the shifting patterns of a snake coiling about its prey, suffocating and deadly, yet maternal and protecting from the rest of the world. None can penetrate these meditations; no urban spectacle can break the spell. When the spirit inside turns itself wholly within, is it with any wonder then the body should be transported, almost corpse-like, to a place of much importance?

The black course of Klong San Saep extended either direction under Torpong's feet. His tired body slouched over the bridge's uneven concrete rail. The waters held him transfixed. However much the will-o-wisp lights may have revealed and animated the surface, the emptiness beneath proved too pitch to reawaken any sought for meaning. How long had the volumes of this waterway crept along the slimy bottom? In what unwitnessed hour had the Chao Phraya forsaken its still-born waters into Bangkok's labyrinth of canals? Damned now to soak into the ever-rotting piers.

Torpong's perception became strangely like that of a child's. For that is where he truly thought himself then standing...as a child hiking by himself now in the wooded hills, peering down over the heaven-illuminated rice fields stretching away. The vast vault above burning night upon night, all the more purely upon the motionless floods below. The stars—there—but then not there. For child-hood stars forever sink into slumber and are inevitably hid behind each subsequent dawn's enchanting lights. But then the night-blown trees whisper once again into the marveling infant's ear as he succumbs to the bottomlessly intimate chambers of his own sacred loneliness. For there in that ever-dimming wilderness had the youth grown conscious of his own small body, thinking the more and more: *one must take care of this form; it must be anointed and protected, washed and watched over for signs of creeping malady... one must come to know this receptacle. It is the only thing that's going to carry you through this world.* And there alone, in the unreachable dark, did the mere child (whose mother still called him 'little mouse') first start to chart out the impossible distances between constellations mirrored in reverse......pretending not to hear the slithering rustle down the branch behind his head. If something were to happen at this moment, if some misfortune befell, who would know? His chin, too tense to turn, pulsed and plunged. The night sky spun uncontrollably across the imaginary fields and pulled the lone boy inwards with a fearsome gravity. The axes of the universe wobbling toward the verge of upending...

—His limp aged form plummeted at this very moment. Headfirst over the rail into the canal.

The water felt precisely like a slap across his cheek. Torpong immediately realized his folly. At no point had he feared for his life until he heard another splash behind, which he mistook for a boat. Instead two sets of slender lifting fingers grabbed round his chest from out the waters. They were woman's hands, pulling him into her wet and swollen embrace. It was that trickling, that smiling face, pressed into his wrinkled cheek. Somehow he'd managed to keep his glasses. She was finding this near fatal misstep of his all too funny.

"How lucky!" she shouted into his ear between hot pants, while he spat out putrid water. Yes, Mr Torpong thought, how lucky.

Chapter 31: With Bated Breath and Whispering Humbleness

After your first time, it must be almost difficult to breathe, so hardly can you wait until the next. This was at least Pink's misconception having basically been handed her first substantial occasion for revenge. It hardly mattered who else might fall along the way, she guessed. How else prove one's pitilessness?

Pink studied Somchai from behind watching him run his fingers through his well-manicured locks. Once he was certain of his hair's perfection, which he was without fail, he'd look back cockily over either shoulder to scan the classroom for possible admirers. My god, the depths of such stupidity! When he finally met her eye, she seized the moment with a pregnant wink. Somchai was a bit unready for it: he'd figured Pink was done with him long ago. He flashed her a practiced smile. Pink knew she could count on his vanity winning over commonsense. The fish had obviously bit. So she decided that the further she prolonged the deception, the more satisfying and just would be the payback come its own sweet time. The trick would be to make him feel himself indebted, to feel his whole self obliged to her.

While Pink had undoubtedly since repeated phrases like *her family's name* and *family honor* in an effort to stoke up the required hatred, how did these invocations touch on anything that was critical to Yan? She thought of what he might be doing right now. Probably slouching behind his mathematics book, dreading what subsequent treachery the day might bring. For an instant Pink felt she might lose her resolve. Her plots however had taken on too much shape to include any inconsequential distractions.

Somchai got up to sharpen his pencil (for what piece of actual schoolwork, she couldn't imagine), and Pink jutted her notebook out so he was forced to knock it to the floor. When he bent down to retrieve it, there was no feasible way that even Somchai couldn't notice the baroque doodling of his name filling the page bared open for all the world to admire. Pink had invested some genuine effort into the hearts & unicorns surrounding it. She had to make certain the imbecile got the message.

"Now whose is this? Yours…I believe this is yours," he pursued tediously confidently. Pink looked into his eyes and let a smile do all her answering. Somchai returned the notebook to the desk, closed it for her, then gave it a pert drum roll with his fingertips.

"I'll be at the fountain after class. Usually doing nothing...if you're not doing anything. I'm there E-VER-Y afternoon," stressing each syllable. She feigned a sort of shy glancing away and down.

Nothing more was needed. And here for the first did Pink realize how the avalanche her vengeance had set in motion might also spare her little cousin any further menace.

Chapter 32: Just Like a Little Mouse

For an investigator like Sgt Mongkut, governed as much by his emotions as by any amount of reason, his recent encounter with the beat-up kid proved too enticing. Whenever the routine of patrol allowed, he leveraged every opportunity to drive through Petchburi to do some extra nosing around.

The sergeant's process was methodic. He'd already spent several afternoons outside the local school at the final bell. Amid the flood of students spilling out, he recognized many of the offending characters from the day of the fight. The big kid who'd battled up to the end was there (some pink-haired prom queen hanging from his arm). It was hard to decide where his muscles got most their exercise: in terrorizing the other boys, or in impressing the girls. And over there was the pigtailed brat too who'd stuck her tongue out at Mongkut when he'd turned the corner. As he watched her keep to the sidelines, preying on isolated individuals, he saw how hers was a more surgical approach. How foolishly these two players performed their pantomime, though their methods might differ in the details. It was obvious they understood how to manipulate the rest of the pack, as they bandied them back and forth. Were they conspirators or rivals? How blind they were to the limits of their influence, blind to the clock ticking rapidly over their puny holdings. Within a short duration's surveillance, Mongkut had been able to predict where these two would end up in time.

It wasn't however until the following week when the sergeant finally spotted the boy he'd been looking for skulk out from some bushes, crawl through a low bend in the bars of the back gate, and then down the alley. He was already too far gone to pursue, but now at least Mongkut knew the child's secret. This tiny mouse was obviously making sure to keep his head down low.

The next day the sergeant pre-positioned himself, watching as the last of the students trickled off the campus. The trick was to afford space, for he understood how children are more sensitive to anomalies in their environment. This kid's nerves were definitely pricked. The chase was a slippery one. He must have been utilizing every neighborhood twist and nook and shadow in his repertoire.

Mongkut recalled the slew of shortcuts and hideouts that filled one's childhood. The city still seemed an endless source. But the sergeant was too slow and clumsy and continued to lose trace of the boy over successive afternoons. First it was behind a bookstand spilling over with children. Then it was somewhere in the fumes of an outdoor meat market; then at the bottom of a stairwell from over a canal; among a throng leaving oblations at a spirit tree; inside the maze of footbridges branching off Chitlom station. Still, there seemed an apparent goal in sight, for the running sum of their repeated hunt progressed along a single route.

Come the following Tuesday, he kept pace all the way down Lang Suan only to lose the boy amid a grove of trees inside Lumpini Park.

The sergeant couldn't remember the last time he'd been in Lumpini Park. He'd forgotten how beautiful a spot it really was. The stands of foliage were so tall in spots, from certain vantages you could almost lose sight of the buildings. Whole populations of birds whirling above the wide lawns seemed to have decided this was as much of the city as they needed to see. Smiling joggers strode past, engrossed in their own worlds. Here and there couples warmed intimate plots of grass beneath the shade of the leaves. Of all places, the sergeant never expected the goose-chase to end up here. He looked up into the paling blue sky. Evening was coming soon. Still, not a cloud up there. What beautiful colors.

This was when a small tennis shoe came dangling from the branches overhead. Mongkut retreated back cautiously until he was behind a nearby palm then simply watched. Occasionally the foot would swing, but otherwise nothing else, no sign of a change in position. What was the boy gazing on from up there? What did he spy upon the horizon?

The cool twilight settled quietly as the park began to empty. The sergeant patiently waited it out.

He'd chased city critters throughout his infancy: dogs and cats and pigeons and rats and geckos. The human game he later learned to track, were they really any different in nature? Frightened animals hide for a reason. So long as Mongkut remained back without becoming the prominent threat, it was only a matter of time before the real predator came slithering out from its cove to reveal its hideous fangs.

Chapter 33: A Day You'll Never Forget

They say your wedding day is one you will never forget, one whose greatest meaning will only be revealed to you when you are gray and trembling and on your deathbed. Finding himself now somewhere squarely in between those two of life's milestones, Mr Torpong could no more recall what was so significantly unforgettable about that day the two of them were betrothed.

Perhaps Torpong really was in some perpetual state of disbelief over Saengdao having accepted his proposal. After they'd gotten past her unhesitating "Yes!", one thing just seemed to lead to another.

He could still remember the explanations the astrologers would produce in assigning the date and hour for the wedding. Imagine explaining to him about the position of the planets and the stars. He could also remember how Saengdao fretted over every detail while insisting on handling the labyrinthine preparations all herself. And he remembered the night before the final ceremony, how nervous he'd felt in front of the monks holding the white string encircling them. Throughout their blessing, he watched the flowers bobbing in their bowl of sacred water upon the ground, wondering over their meaning. Legs crossed, the monks then stretched out their fingers for the obligatory envelopes of cash.

Torpong also vividly remembered plodding to his bride's house the next day—the day of the actual wedding—in the hot sun, by himself. The money he symbolically surrendered to Saengdao's sisters and nieces along the way and in front of her house was about the total sum he had left to contribute after having splurged on a modest ring. It was the bride's family, otherwise, who paid for what was to be a lavish and well-attended event. Torpong was glad the ceremony was over quickly and that soon enough the guests were finished pouring holy water over their hands from shells.

So much family, so many bows. None of the relatives or friends was his. If only his parents had survived, his mother would've seen he'd finally met somebody.

There came a point he overhead a pack of guests whisper how the bride was marrying beneath her rank. It made Torpong pity Saengdao more than it did himself. But the fleeting emotion eventually submerged beneath the onslaught of feasting, small-talk and dancing, of which there was no telling when any of it'd ever end. And then before you knew it, his mother-in-law was reminding him to "lock the door" when she was the last to leave. Torpong and Saengdao agreed they were both too tired from the celebration and went right to sleep without another word. Torpong's last thought that night was how he hoped he'd never have to attend another wedding.

*

Surely he was more or less the same person since. How much can one fundamentally alter, howsoever many the years conjoined? Would things have been any different if he'd grown old alone? Life as it pretty much is continues on and on. Still, there are the slight inevitable changes that married life bestows along its way.

The first real shift in habits was a newly fostered awareness of the appearance and smell of his body. During their honeymoon, Saengdao introduced him to a bevy of lotions and tonics. His skin was notably smoother anymore; the wrinkles beneath his eyes were largely gone. His hair was always dyed and kempt, his fingernails closely clipped. She also talked him into getting contact lenses so she could see his face more clearly. (He kept his glasses tucked away still though, just in case.) She liked her husband when he was fragrant and smooth and trim and unobscured, and often let him know. Most of all it was her repeated smiles that helped to reinforce this new regime.

Over time Torpong also learned how to appreciate a more refined cuisine, and how to distinguish the stringencies of different wines one washes it down the lips with. Hadn't their courtship essentially developed over the course of many dinners? (Saengdao would say it was she that'd done all the wooing.) Ever since, they made repeated rounds of all the plushest restaurants. Their meals commenced with just the two of them, but they were eventually surrounded by a group of acquaintances asking to join their table. One evening might include a soap opera star, another a senior lieutenant. Everyone was more than willing to contribute their own fair share to the conversation, except for Mr Torpong, who was content to listen to his wife extolling upon such topics as the digestive virtues of lemongrass, or the healing properties of jade. He loved to watch the way her black curls whisked in unison with her head across her shoulders, the way her eyes danced between the crowd's enraptured glances. Her smile might turn mischievous, or snide at times, then into a boisterous childish outburst. Her ardor was exhilarating. It simply made Torpong feel young again.

As he took another sip of wine and let his tongue bathe in the settling bitterness, he thought to himself how strange that marriage could unlock these countless vistas onto the universe of Bangkok's social elite. It was a world he thought he'd never witness. A world that showed no limit.

*

After the death of their premature daughter, Saengdao changed.

She was too proud to don grief outwardly. Torpong knew she thought it made her look weak, but he felt the gravity nonetheless.

"Now there's part they never tell you. One never quite attains the same height of yearning as when one's listening," she argued one night in bed as they listened to a performance of Mozart's '*Voi che sapete*' over the radio. "Once the music's ended, you're left hung out to dry."

How could Torpong sincerely refute his wife on this point? He'd merely mentioned how sad yet joyful the aria was. As he lay in bed, his wife asleep now, he thought, "...*vedete s'io l'ho nel cor*... Isn't that the crux of the song, that Cherubino shows himself to be fully aware of what love is though he believes himself ignorant? That it's the yearning and the never being satisfied that's the hallmark of love...*Ch'ora e diletto, ch'ora e martir*...not the suffering that redeems the desire...*Ma pur mi piace languir cosi*...but the reaching, the unmet desire...*Ricerco un bene fuori di me*... Otherwise why would we have lain awake, together, so many nights ago. So many, sleepless with excitement for our unborn child? *Ricerco un bene fuori di me.* Where have those nights flown to? *s'io l'ho nel cor..."*

*

Somewhere however in that repeating hour of troubled slumber, somewhere throughout so many nights accumulated in that one shared bed, relief did come to Torpong. One can only ask an unanswered question so many times before another obsession will eventually take its place.

Torpong began to dream he was another person.

Night after night he dreamt he was Nehn Kaeo to be exact. And who was Nehn Kaeo you ask? Nehn Kaeo was a scholar monk. From first sight (if one can speak like this about such matters), Torpong knew he liked and could trust this persona inhabiting his dreams, this other self. For the experience of witnessing his own dreams through the vehicle of another retained many of the same initial uncertainties and uncomfortableness as when we meet a stranger. Though this imaginary monk behaved much like the dreamer often did himself, once Torpong had awoken, there remained something unmistakably unknown about Nehn Kaeo, something impenetrable about his existence. There was an inscrutable schism, a faint yet vital hue to Torpong's subconscious creation which couldn't endure surfacing into the real world's dispelling light.

Throughout the waking hours of his days, Torpong found himself impatient to rush right back to bed, to this other rich and more inviting realm. Why must tonight be so far off, he asked himself at the breakfast table. But the daydreamer now gazing into his tea felt always too embarrassed, or maybe selfish, to mention anything to his wife sitting just opposite.

Besides, the details he found most fascinating would've sounded idiotic if he'd spoken them aloud. It wasn't as if Nehn Kaeo was a great adventurer or inspired mystic. Indeed within the make-believe history of Torpong's dreams, Kaeo's only claim to fame was an apparent rebuke from the monkhood's patriarchs.

Kaeo was a historian of the visual arts: his specialty late 18th-century painting. And he would unheededly claim unto his dying day that, in one particular specimen of an anonymous work from the Chiang Mai period, he'd found an imperfection that brought into question the entire canonized sequence of the Wetsandon Chadok cycle. It's no wonder his research wrinkled more than a few shaved-headed brows.

The Maha Wetsandon Chadok tale, or the *Great Birth* as it is generally known, follows the life of Prince Wetsandon, the final incarnation of Lord Buddha before becoming the Buddha. The prince was a man of virtue so absolute and pure, he never once hesitated to relinquish every last possession (including his wife and two children). And over time, as his tale's become incorporated into the Dhamma, artist and poet alike have chosen to depict the prince's biography in similar fashion: in thirteen emblematic episodes.

Among the painters however, a unique and curious tradition came about that has no root within religious doctrine. No one can say from where or when the superstition originated, but even today, whenever the aspiring artist sits down to illustrate the thirteen scenes, whether on paper or cloth or walls of stone, the same old fabled curse perforce bedevils his imagination, even today in these skeptical times. For it's said that if the painter completes the full thirteen-fold cycle, upon the instant he lays that final stroke, an incontrollable madness will infect his brain until he raves just like a dying beast. Which is why, if you examine closely, you will invariably find hidden in one of the thirteen paintings some unfinished element. An uncompleted cloud or temple column for instance.

The journey of the art historian, as that of any historian, is a planned descent into quicksand: the more arduously one claws things up into the light, the faster the floor dissolves beneath one's feet. Perhaps it was this inherent paradox of such an intellectual pursuit, realized as it was merely in his dreams, that made it so easy for Torpong to elaborate upon these fictions of his mind.

Just as the admiring student might try to reenact how a master draftsman applied his strokes, Torpong loved sitting back and observing Kaeo—the habits of his scholarship, the rhythm of his research—and trying to guess the monk's unspoken hunches and conclusions. Torpong might presume to know each single last one of Nehn Kaeo's thoughts: he was the dreamer after all. But more than any tangible discovery or result, Torpong learned to savor every next step throughout the whole monk's life, like the chapters of a novel. There had been the day they first shaved Kaeo's boyish head with a straightedge. And then the day he stepped, with cocksure authority, over the lintel into the temple's most sacred collection. Then at last the stewing shame of being demoted back to initiate in the budding of a devout and honorable career.

Yet it wasn't until recently, not until having traced for so many nights the permutations of the monk's ongoing studies, having gazed through Kaeo's eyes upon the same thirteen imaginary sheets with their timeworn colors, that Torpong began to believe he was getting close to seeing the same thing his alter ego saw with such clarity. Closer to being able to fix his vision upon the one select painting's elusive lacuna. While he slept, Torpong was sure he could envision all at once the cycle in its complete perfection. Come morning, staring at the film spinning atop his tea once more, nothing but the artwork's shallowest meaning was ever retrievable. Which of the thirteen was it? No matter how deeply he peered into his cup, Torpong couldn't decide.

*

His frequent distractions didn't irritate Saengdao as much as he might have expected. The truth was she'd always had far too many of her own to fret about. The husband knew his wife worked hard. He could hear her voice from behind her office door at all hours of the night once she'd returned from work, her directives stern but collected.

Torpong had a tentative concept of the nature of her job. He had tried early on to pry, but she never wanted to talk to him about it at length, and so he gave up. Perhaps she thought he wouldn't understand. She was involved with city development, but not under the employment of the government. Lots and lots of numbers representing lots of money—that's the gist of what Torpong knew. On the occasions he entered her office, all he found were reams of budget reports and amortization tables. What was confirmed in all those computations was confirmed at home: business must be on a constant climb, because he saw less and less of Saengdao.

Happily her preoccupation afforded Torpong time to sit and to ponder, undisturbed. What else did he have to do? He'd quit his own post the first year of their marriage;

there simply wasn't a need now for the tiny income. He hadn't genuinely minded, though he sometimes wished he'd kept his resolution to devote his freedom to pursuing some form of self-enrichment. Sure, he loved to dally. He dallied and he dallied in subject after subject, but never very profoundly before hurrying onto the next. Each new but never finished book only opened unto a dozen others. In the end even his hobby of astronomy fell by the wayside, like a neglected hound unfed so long it just might snap if approached too closely. It all seemed like too much labor anymore. He hardly had the energy to pace their apartment's many rooms, in his robe and sipping tea, at any given hour. At least the fantasies of his dreams sustained him through these quiet days.

*

One afternoon he mustered the resolve to straighten out a closet full of old junk. Atop the highest shelf he found the white banner that had briefly hung above their daughter's crib: on the one side, the child's mischievous mae-sue with its hideous pink skin; on the other, Tao Wessuwan, King of the Giants. Not even the dreaded Tao Wessuwan had been able to ward off the death of their baby, who passed before they could officially name her. Lek. That is what Torpong always wanted to nickname her.

As the father sat slumped on the floor in the corner of the room, sobbing into the cloth crumpled in his fists, Saengdao entered. She looked shocked by his raw emotion but was quick to regain composure. With an almost mechanical simplicity, she turned and withdrew straight off and behind the latching door of her office. Torpong sat paralyzed, listening intently through the pulse of his own heartbeat, too terrified to know what to do. But after a few laden minutes, he at last heard his wife upon the phone again, straight back to work.

Did Torpong suspect her first thought had been that she didn't have time for this? That she didn't want to have to endure it all over again?

He realized that he loved her because she pitied him. He knew she did not think she pitied him, but she did. He knew she only loved him because she pitied him. And he loved her because she pitied him.

Torpong vowed to never mention another thing.

Chapter 34: A Lesson in Life

"And in this way is every one of your growing lives, down to the count of the hairs on your head, already plotted out in advance through the mystery of these two microscopic, million-manifold, complementarily intertwining strands," Professor Nagani brought today's biological lecture to an intellectual climax with. The statement's bold philosophic implications, along with its grosser scientific misrepresentations, were wholly lost on his late-afternoon audience. Clearly the professor's peculiar breed of determinism was wasted on the youth of today. Had Mr Nagani instead mentioned something about 'fate' or 'destiny', it might have been a different story. His students might have better understood the underlying menace. "DNA's true miracle, then, depends on if and when these genes become expressed."

Pink slouched in her desk, cognizant of the flow of words, but looking out the window instead, watching Fah's class in the courtyard doing calisthenics. Unlike the remainder of her schoolmates, Fah looked like she was genuinely enjoying the exercises. Her legs appeared as if to dance upon the wind beneath her floating skirt; those two pigtails flapping in rhythm above either corner of her panting smile, not another care in the world. Not a care about her precipitating unpopularity at school. Nor about the fact every member of the faculty was eagerly awaiting the day she'd finally make that critical mistake that'd get her kicked out for good. Nor at any time did Fah outwardly betray the slightest jot of compunction.

Pink recalled catching Fah through the classroom window last week pilfering Nagani's desk. Fah had looked up to Pink briefly, then went right back to her handiwork.

As Pink now watched Fah's jumping, gleeful body, it reminded her of herself at that age. And reflecting on this fancied image of her own youth, Pink realized Fah was in fact precisely the opposite of what everyone accused her of—she was perfectly innocent. An almost animal-like ignorance left her impugn, made her free. There was no conception of crime in Fah's unchecked hunger and impulse. It was clear to anybody with an understanding of the disciplinary consequences that follow such heights of rebeliousness, that Fah was a dangerous person with whom to get entangled. Her existence necessarily complicated matters.

*

Later that day Pink caught Yan's backside skulking round the corner as she and Somchai entered the courtyard arm-in-arm. It'd been days since she'd so much as teased her little cousin. However Somchai quickly interrupted the tender thought with a kiss to Pink's unready lips.

"Not now, you idiot!"

"Relax, sweet cheeks. Everybody knows." Mr Nagani had warned them loudly in the halls that he'd notify their parents if he caught them at it again.

"I don't doubt it. Still I'm hardly trying to live up to everybody's expectations. Besides, you'll get in trouble at home next time," she protested as she nudged him away.

Pink understood the chief allure for Somchai was that she was older. A good number of her coconspirators were beginning to question the sanity of what was essentially suicide to Pink's social status, of the heaps of gossip she'd endure all in the name of justice. None of her retinue had seen through Pink's moral rhetoric. None realized what she sought wasn't entirely justice.

"My father wouldn't give two shits. He's too busy. He was the same way, you know. Or so that's what my aunts would have me believe, though I can't fucking imagine it."

Pink had heard this litany before. She found it almost unconscionable how Somchai excused his own behavior due to his father's precedent. It was true his dad was totally absent. Not even when she and Somchai used to hang out back when they were kids did she remember meeting the patriarch in question. Instead he was off running his business, leaving his mark on this world as a string of gutted skyscrapers across the city, and overflowing all the appropriate coffers. Simply put, his dad's company Empire Reclamation & Scrap was one of those family enterprises that had recognized opportunity in cleaning up the pieces after '97 and magically prospered ever since.

So you'd think all this good fortune would have altered the fate of its only living son, the heir to the throne if you will. But beyond a superficial heap-load of new clothes and toys, it hadn't. Pink couldn't understand why Somchai had decided to stay in Petchburi while his parents resided in an apartment in Sukhumvit now. He visited there weekends, but come the school week, here he remained, living with Fah and his three aunts in his old home, out of his parents' hair. This was one thing Pink had to admit: Somchai had stayed true to himself throughout his family's meteoric ascent up the socio-economic ladder. He was still the same vain and sex-crazed Somchai.

"Like father, like son. That's what I say," she mocked.

"You only wish I were that depraved. You'll have to scrape deeper into the barrel than me if that's what you're after."

"Oh, you do yourself an injustice. You're plenty deep."
Pink couldn't help but laugh at her jibe. Somchai laughed
in return. At least he could laugh at himself too. It was
hard to imagine how such a boy, who could be so cruel
to others, could also muster the wit when the occasion
demanded. His subsequently fitful seducing however
barely registered with Pink, whose mind began to wander.
It wandered as it had earlier in class, not to the mechanics
of her plan for Somchai, but to something uncertain and
amazingly different.

Chapter 35: The Other Path

Try as you might, the city will not so easily let your existence slip between its fingers. Too often do we forget how much the world depends upon our very presence. There are the jarring morning alarm clocks that need to get shut off. There's the familiar weekday uniform waiting to be filled and buttoned, formed over time to just your size it seems. There is a meal someone might have made for you without having thought twice about it. There are the hundreds of passersby who're destined to find a thousand opaque and transient meanings in your passing glance. There are cars that turn or brake to avoid crushing a fellow human being, who sometimes happens to be you. There are the peers who forget to joke behind your back unless they actually see you. Your desk empty and waiting. Then there are the many lists with many instances of your name that need to be checked off or left unchecked. That is simply the beginning of your daily dose.

But in the hour when that final school bell rings, once you can quietly escape all the places people recognize you, then and only then can you immerse yourself in that ephemeral solace of anonymity. While it sometimes serves to remind, the city is good at helping to forget in equal measure.

It's difficult to tell how far and deep Yan had managed to travel into this elusive eremitism, the painful routine intervals between his solitudes felt like a mere resurfacing nightmare anymore. It'd gotten to the point Yan hated to even hear his name spoken, that alone proving too much of an impediment to a retreat from his existential duty. But if he kept his mouth shut and his head down, it'd only be a matter of time before he could escape back into the beauty of his newborn loneliness.

During those hours when no one knew him, Yan was free to do whatever and go whereever he liked. One thing he was sure of, he was done returning to Lumpini Park.

There were times when he'd walk as straight a line as Bangkok allows until the afternoon had turned to evening. Once he allowed himself to turn back toward Petchburi, the distance his feet had paced could not exhaust his spirit's eagerness to witness the path again, but this time by the dancing lights of night and in reverse.

This retracing of his steps afforded Yan an unexpected perspective on the day's trek into new frontiers. What he thought had been a more or less straight route turned out in truth to have contained a thousand turns and idle digressions. Here, he remembered, had been the cart tipped and spilling flowers, cleaned up and long departed since. Here was where he'd surreptitiously crossed the street in order to avoid the monks. Here's where that short old lady had made him laugh by pretending she was chasing him like a chicken with her cane. Crazy old lady! Past what he could still only conceive to be Toi's father's restaurant, bypassed determinedly each time. And there was the blind alley, more shadowy yet, out of which that scrappy dog had come snapping madly. Was the beast there still tonight? Slumbering hopefully.

The memories attained a greater clarity, as if he were watching them unfold for the first time. So easy did it seem now to string together each inch of that journey under the analytic microscope, until he could piece together every minute and banal detail of that revisited story, which he'd carry inside him like a secret, infinitely faceted gem.

Yan always made it into bed before his mother returned. Beneath his sheets, he could at last relax and resign himself to the fact that sleep might erode away that buried treasure for good.

Chapter 36: The Start of Trouble

"You really ought to just plumb drop the case, sir."

"You forget I was never assigned it," Mongkut told the meddlesome intern transporting a stack of files the opposite direction up the staircase. Someone had figured out he'd been lurking around the school in Petchburi, and now he was the laughingstock of the department.

He was sure they were calling him a pervert behind his back. Not that the raillery rattled him much. This was normal human behavior, to leap headlong into cruelty once it's been socially sanctioned. He fully understood that it was nothing personal they were harboring against him: Mongkut was simply the readiest scapegoat at hand. But it is exceedingly difficult for a scapegoat to stay inconspicuous. Fortunately it'd also be natural for his workmates to eventually stray their aim away and onto the next unfortunate soul to come tripping along. Still, if word got round to any of the locals, his investigation in Petchburi might be seriously compromised.

Besides, he'd lost complete track of the boy several days back. What a ridiculous old fool he'd been, falling asleep like that waiting and watching the kid up in the tree at the park. Despite the sergeant's sharpest efforts, he hadn't been able to spot the child along the usual route since.

So he decided his energy might be better spent finally interviewing the dead kid's parents. It had been over a week since the drowning and Mongkut felt enough time had passed for them to have recovered from the burdens of the funeral and to start to settle into their own private lives and private grief.

*

When he came to the entrance of the apartment, there were a couple of unkempt toddlers smacking the apartment's cracked staircase with sticks. Their presumed mother watched complacently from the shade of the doorway. Mongkut told her who he was and who he wanted to see. He repeated the names after she shook her head, thinking she didn't hear him over the traffic and the kids. She shook no again.

"No one by that name lives here, sir."

"And you don't recognize either the sister's or the brother's name?"

She wrinkled her nose and shrugged her shoulders. The mom then turned to scold the children for jumping out too close to the street and the sergeant helped corral them back to safety with some silly whistles and playful waving of his arms. When he lifted his glance away from their giggling faces, Mongkut noticed in the distance the very kid he'd been following dash across the street.

Sgt Mongkut stepped briskly to, scanning the far sidewalk for another glimpse of that timid face. When he reached Petchburi Road, he thought he saw him crossing the footbridge and looking back. The sergeant dashed straight into traffic to try and shorten the gap without considering how the subsequent squealing of tires and wailing of horns was sure to draw attention. A startled merchant abandoned his storefront to meet him halfway. Mongkut bowed and thanked the concerned Samaritan for helping him across, then resumed his chase up toward the canal. He was certain it was the top of the kid's head just dipping beyond the crest of the bridge.

Mongkut quickened his pace in order to surmount the staircase before the boy could disappear on the other side. Surely it was only a matter of a couple blocks before he overtook him and confronted him at last. So closely did the sergeant have to watch that his shuffling, sweating feet didn't trip upon the steep steps, when he glanced upward to see if he was gaining, he never once saw coming the stone-hard object that cracked his right eye-socket and knocked him stumbling back—down into the footless crashing black, like a loosed sack of coconuts!

There was no kind-hearted citizen around this time to aid the poor soul flat on his back. He mistook the juice spilling from the split green coconut behind his pulsing head to be his own blood. A small, pigtailed silhouette stepped forward into the splinter of sun blinding his left eye.

"He's not the only one, freak! Yan's not the only one being followed!" the girl's sharp words mocked from high atop the stairs. She held something small before her face for a moment. Then her black shape bobbed off.

The addled Mongkut couldn't grasp what she'd meant. Was this boy's name Yan too...just like the one who'd drowned?

Chapter 37: The Golden Boy

…not the smallest atom stirs or lives in matter, but has
its cunning duplicate in mind.

–Moby-Dick

If you want nothing less than a guarantee, then the
amulet must be 100% authentic. Not all articles of
magic are what they pretend, running the risk of instilling
a false sense of confidence at the moment when true faith
is most critical. An unshakable level of protection, too,
invariably requires a not insignificant level of compen-
sation. The usual care and attention any of your lower
caliber charms might recommend—the devoted polish-
ing, offerings of foodstuffs, whispering to from time to
time—these rituals are not enough for the highest rank of
spirits. A tried commitment alone will appease, a degree
of sacrifice perhaps one wouldn't dare contemplate under
less dire circumstances. But for the soul dogged by disaster after disaster, that act of finally crossing the threshold
into surrender no longer poses any second thought. Such
clientele expect some reassurance they're being handed

only the absolute best in exchange for their rather sizably rendered sum.

Of course we're merely discussing the *leasing* of the necessary charm. Never speculate it otherwise than completely unconscionable to talk in terms of 'owning' one. The choice you will soon weigh, the lifelong bargain you're going to have to decide whether or not to embark upon is of such an existentially decisive nature, who'd dare offend the purity of the pact by fantasizing ever owning an amulet? The spirit inside is an eternal force— but woe unto all of history's wearers! It goes without saying, none can claim down the road they hadn't been amply warned.

We also ought to agree further on at least one clear ontological principle: everything upon this blessed earth must find its own beginning. Yet the origin of each last thing, alive or not, however complex or simple, is shrouded in impenetrable darkness. You also are of this darkness, I say, and it is as much defined in you.

And so why not just humor that natural curiosity and try this exercise on for size? The next time you find yourself in the old city center, browsing the patchwork of blankets along the sidewalk and the laden makeshift stalls, pop your head into one of the more reputable establishments, if only to give your brow some respite from the noonday sun. Greet its smiling proprietor at the entrance with a similarly humble bow. Leave the splutter of the streets behind. Let the nearby crumple and clink of counted bills and coins go unnoticed. Let the rest of the world vanish from your mind. Bring your face down close to better glimpse the wares beneath your faint reflection upon the showcase. Take a deep breath and, focused now, peruse at leisure the array beneath your nose. Then just select, randomly perhaps, one of those varied specimens at rest inside its own flocked bin. And ask yourself this one pre-liminary question: how is it the mystery of what we call 'spirit' came to reside within this tiny carven form? What hand could've brought about the transubstantiation?

They say the monks who wield such gifts are guided by forces outside their comprehension, and amulet-mak-ers are among the most enlightened and holiest of men. There's no disputing they've paid their dues: the hours of meditation; the onslaught of a thousand ghosts through the deep of night; temptation lurking under every leaf and rock. Yet when it comes time to bring tool to metal, clay or to stone, the monk cannot say whence inspiration reaches hand. But reach his hand it must.

Nor should the *animus* be sought exclusively inside the substance from which the amulet's wrought. True, upon closer inspection that stone or clay or metal too is animate. It too has lived a life, albeit unimaginable in scope beneath millennia of earth. Since the firmament was born, each atom has lain quietly, slowly metamorphosing, patiently waiting to be dug from beneath the chosen monk's or sage's wandering feet. Solely in the maker's illuminated eye is the accumulation of time uncovered through the organic twists and turns of the mineral's texture, weight and hue. Something inherent in the matter, something in its properties guides the artificer as he searches for its future form, be it depiction of bird or snake or phallus or monk or king or angel or Lord Buddha Himself. Indeed there usually is an admixture of elements too, which can prove more efficacious still. But whether compound or unalloyed, in the end, the amulet's magic relies upon these two participants: the maker's grasp, and his beloved materials. Without this marriage, the spirit of the charm could never find its way to light. Only somewhere in-between and in the shadow, only through that narrow passage between mind and manifestation can that whispering wind from beyond enter our world.

I feel I know you well enough by now to share it's one of Bangkok's best-kept secrets that the greatest amulets were carved by unknown hands. All too often those other pieces associated with notable monks fetch the highest price. Let's face it, if there's a captivating biography or legend to accompany, this can't hurt a charm's appeal. But accrediting one recognizable name typically distorts the reality of an amulet's creation. More frequently the power is summoned by a roomful of the devout chanting prayer into the figurine's ears, to sing it from its slumber. Sometimes the charm is consecrated by ashes from the burning of the monastery's most ancient texts, scholars' near million late-night hours lost. For that is what the spirit inside demands—rash life! It demands the pangs of birth, the hypnotics of song, destruction of the past, the rapture of being idolized. Without such indulgences, let's call them, could the spirit adequately comprehend how best to serve? Would it know how to read the outward display of our own desires and fears? Would it recognize the lust for romance or wealth or victory or fame? By what other means could the article dare claim to ward off death?

…Yes, we amulets do fear death…

Or perhaps more appropriately, we do recall what it once meant to fear it. Many of us still can taste its bitter grit.

The wanderers of the spirit world consort both far and wide. Collectively we've figured out exactly that which one forgets at rebirth—all death's tricks and traps. Thus are we able to snatch our wearer from its clutch, because we've studied death's variations almost flawlessly. Believe me, we remember. What lifelong passion consumes one's heart more than death? Yet whatever the particular shade or scent, we spirits have seen and categorized it. Or if some soul's is destined yet to be an unparalleled death, then it's only a matter of time before we get to savor it at last and learn. In sum, this is the expertise we bring to the transaction.

But before we go ahead and wrap things up, I must warn you of a couple additional things (and eventually also confess). In a number of case studies, some adverse side-effects have been spotted. A wearer or two may have come down with one or two not negligible symptoms. Rest assured however; the ailments were only ever of the mind:

The first affliction seems to settle in when, though emphatically discouraged from the start, the wearer over-indulges the magic, trusting unswervingly to the point of lunacy. Perhaps some magnetism innate to the amulet paralyzes all commonsense. To be exact, these unfortunate souls come to disdain everything except themselves, believing themselves untouchable by an inconsequential world. It is in fact a strain of nihilism that shrugs off every last phenomenon as if it were merely the next in an infinite chain of impotent chance. Inexcusable idolatry! Death always catches up. Do not fall prey to this temptation.

On the other side of the coin you'll find the converse misconception, yet it is more curious still. This poor lot, though they go through all the motions—seek consultation on the proper charm, save the extra funds to lease a finer specimen, and lastly reenact the prescribed rituals day in and out— secretly they still cannot bring themselves to believe, no matter how hard they try, despite all signs of proof. Maybe there was an incident when the amulet appeared to fail in its duties, and faith was lost hereafter. Yet really can one ever blame the charm? Who in fact was the first to stray? And still this unhappy sort continues to disingenuously don the amulet, as a topic for conversation at best, like all the other disposable trifles to which they turn instead to sooth their cares. Useless ornaments to flatter transience. Here again it all smacks of a childish egomania with no insight into more 'grownup' matters. Sadly this latter mania is in the ascendant. But once again, death always catches up.

I swear I speak intelligently upon such matters. I too have lived a life, however brief. But now also has courteous death come and opened up all life's doors. And since I finally have your undivided attention, indulge me just a bit more and bring the amulet closer to your eye. Don't be afraid to ask: "What is this piece here? This charming little one formed like a child at ease, legs crossed. How is it called? It looks nearly too rich in tone to be of even gold. What never before seen material is it crafted from?"

Charming little me? I am made from the most taboo of substances and arts. Without consent I've been brought back into this world by purest Saiyasart—pure blackest magic. I am the firstborn of death. I am the Golden Boy.

As the good shop owner notes, I hunger for offerings of eggs and only ask you pull the corners of my frozen smile with playful jokes whispered in my ear from time to time. You clearly see how such a name as mine is a good omen. My miniature round and grinning face brings such a flitting joy to gaze upon. But before you make your final decision, I should probably also mention to you about, well, the sordidness of my origin. But oh— it's the sordidness that's my sanctity! For me, the spirit's liberation from suffering came near as quick as birth into its corporeal bondage. I died before I could recall how to become impure, because so long ago I died within my mother's womb. My life had passed within a blinking of her tearful eye.

I will not say just how it was the Ruesi freed me from my natal tomb. Perhaps it was the minuteness of my life, my next-to-nothingness that summoned that visionary ascetic from out of the wilderness to take and nurture me and hold me sacred. (For no ordained monk would dare touch such forbidden arts.) Thus was my tiny corpse then hastily borne to the nearest cemetery in the dead of night, where it was set ablaze within a holy flame until completely desiccated. Not one blot from my weak heart remains. And while the delicate charred bones still glowed

with an undying heat, with tender brush did the chanting mage apply quivering leaf after gold leaf to my fire-
cleansed shape until—second birth arrived!

Can you not see through to the unimaginable beauty
beneath my form's reflecting foil? Rarely do I begrudge
the brutal act of defilement my body had to undergo. Did
not the Lord Buddha Himself touch down his hand and
call on Mother Earth to bear witness? This time creation
is invulnerable. From an existence of greatest fragility to
that of an immortal.

Immortal, that is, so long as you consent. As long as
some living soul agrees to participate. If there is but a
remnant of belief, even undeclared or hardly recognized,
is that not the selfsame secret the desperate artificer must
forever keep, especially from himself—that his creation
is pure artifice?

You tell me, you who now have heard my pitch, you
who looked so skeptical from the very start. Is there not
some unseen wound in your heart that's tacitly compelled
to accept what I speak, if only from revulsion? Call it
doubt if you must...a momentary disbelief in your otherwise unassailable doubt. Doubt too will do for belief
these days. If I can be made to acknowledge a creature
whose being is as fantastic and (forgive the term) absurd
as yours, why should you be so reluctant to accept the
truth of mine? Look at how entranced you are with your

own impossible life, how much you believe in all its grimy details. It's a wonder you had the slightest inclination to stop and take a closer peek, so preoccupied were you with whatever it was you'd been daydreaming about. Is it not maybe even more difficult to believe in that little fleeting dream that filled your head just then? Look at you—you can't even recall from what imagined spot you inadvertently left off.

But if you still refuse, you wouldn't be the first to walk away and back into the deadly whorl of the city streets empty-handed, unprotected. Or do I maybe sense you reaching down and for your wallet? Indeed is it not already too late? Haven't we found ourselves too far along? Any opportunity to object seems almost to have gone and flown long down the ageless river flowing through the city just outside. So what that, over what happens to the wearer after death, we amulets have no dominion?

If on the other hand this all just sounds a bit involved or overwhelming, maybe your time would have been better spent at Weekend Market.

Chapter 38: And On

Sooner or later this conversation was going to have to find its way to an end, Saengdao kept telling herself. It made her already weary torso sag the more heavily into the hard chair to have to listen to her husband's endless blather. Was this any kind of gratitude? Was this her due reward for all the long hours of work: to have to listen to Torpong wind his way through an endless series of totally unrelated topics? English gardens, binary code, silk-making, evolutionary biology. Was this how he squandered the days of uninterrupted leisure Saengdao had always insisted he deserved? Why had he taken to wearing those stupid glasses again? What could Torpong possibly know or think he had to say about evolution?

The worst aspect was she never put up much resistance, never once told him to just shut up. Her only hope was to limit her participation in order not to fuel the prattle. Why didn't he talk about the stars anymore? She used to love to listen to him teach her all about the stars. He'd get such a look in his eyes. She thought back to the first time he'd accompanied her on a plane. It was his first flight ever, to Seoul she recalled. He was nervous beforehand when she'd told him they'd be flying over the ocean. It was night. How sweet to see him shuffle around the empty seats in first-class like an excited boy trying to orientate himself. He said it was difficult to figure their position amid the constellations swimming up so high.

That rare magical perspective of seeing the world through another's eyes, a particular point-of-view she'd once found so disarming, still rippled within her memory. Had her husband ever thought about how she saw things? Had he not benefited from her in any similarly enduring way? Saengdao couldn't remember the last time he'd touched the telescope she bought him for their third anniversary. The stupid instrument just sat out there haphazardly cocked and frozen on the balcony anymore.

*

This was only the tip of the iceberg. Look at what happened just last week.

She'd thought it would be good for him to get out and socialize rather than being cooped up in their apartment like he usually was. So Saengdao decided to turn a business obligation showing a couple American bankers around Bangkok into an opportunity for her husband to interact with other people. She knew the bankers well; they were both friendly, if not slightly too friendly sometimes. But they would respect and be overtly kind in Torpong's presence. Besides, she knew her husband's English was more than passable, so he had no excuse. In the end, he was unable to find a single good one for not attending. Which was unfortunate, considering how everything turned out.

Saengdao had them all driven to the Grand Palace. Torpong didn't say a word the whole ride there. Throughout the tour, he kept falling behind. Then at one point Saengdao had to double-back to find him.

He was standing in front of one of the far hall's murals. The painting was of a figure asleep. A peaceful mask adorned the face of the creature, for a creature it must have been with that black-blue skin and those hideous pointed teeth. Its golden breastplate had fractured with the stone, revealing how long the monster had slept frozen upon the wall there. What had it dreamt of so devoutly throughout the ages? A tranquil sea and sky stretching far behind.

Torpong just stood there smiling and staring at the mural, barely noticing Saengdao. She told him to just please not wander from this spot while she took her clients to see the Emerald Buddha. He wasn't there when she returned.

Saengdao spent at least half an hour walking and scanning the entire grounds of the palace. At last she had to apologize to her clients and called the car to take them back to their hotel. She was going to kill her husband once she located him. For over an hour more she pounded the long boulevards querying strangers if they'd seen anyone resembling Torpong. Fuck, how to describe him? You know…glasses! She stopped asking because it made her sound like such an idiot.

Evening was beginning to fall when she spotted the back of his head inside an amulet shop. Saengdao stormed in yelling and swearing at her husband, at the shopkeeper. She made sure he hadn't spent any money and then dragged him out to the street by the shoulder of his jacket and down to the corner where she hailed a cab. The ride was completely silent as was the elevator ride to their apartment. Once Saengdao had shut and latched the front door behind, she pushed Torpong down into a kitchen chair and stated her position straightly.

"If I ever catch you in the amulet market again, if I ever find you wasting my money on that shit, I'll cut your balls off—then you can wear *those* around your neck!"

Why didn't he have anything to say for himself? He just sat there, his lower teeth just perceptible behind a thin tense grin. You could read the terror in his eyes. Saengdao didn't know how to respond to that stupid, inscrutable grin, so she turned and disappeared inside her office as resignedly as thunder rumbles off. A familiar silence hung about the kitchen for several minutes before Mr Torpong eventually stood and started pacing, unsure of what to do with himself. He made out the muffled voice of his wife from the other side of the door and tiptoed up and put his ear carefully to, praying she wouldn't hear. Her words echoed flatly in the wooden panel now separating the two.

"...I think he needs to have his head examined."

Chapter 39: More Trouble at Work

What could one really say about it? It was a photo of Sgt Mongkut lying out cold on the concrete below the steps: one side of his face winced and red; one cracked green coconut just above his head. In fact there was something so unusual about the picture's perspective, it made Mongkut's body seem positioned intentionally flat-and-squarely, like a cadaver and (for some reason) a coconut in a medical lecture. One could stare and stare at the strangeness of the image, yet never ascertain the slightest glimpse behind its story.

When Mongkut first saw the photograph awaiting him in the lieutenant's office, he couldn't call to mind the exact moment it represented. He remembered climbing that first stair, and then he remembered seeing the girl with the pigtails lower what he now understood to be a phone. But the unknown span between the blow and the snapshot was a blank. Had anything significant transpired within the interim? Now however was hardly the time to delve into the wrinkled curtains of his own subconscious. The lieutenant's pointed silence demanded a prompt, if not half-sincere response.

Mongkut turned the printout over when he placed it back upon the desk. The gesture was lost on the lieutenant, whose face seemed focused on squeezing out any last affectation of anger. God how Mongkut's swollen eye still throbbed.

"And your question again, sir?" The sergeant hated playing dumb, but he was obviously nonplused by the evidence. He wasn't sure why he should feel guilty for following the boy—he really hadn't done anything wrong. And who's to say anyone besides the girl had made the connection? Yet Mongkut did still taste some hint of shame, which he tried to conceal from the sight of his close friend the lieutenant. "I'm afraid I didn't catch the tail end of it."

"There is no tail end as far as I can see! Have you seen the nonsense piling up around this picture on the internet? If we don't act now, the papers will be onboard. Remember, you weren't assigned the case in the first place. Don't tell me you'd been drinking. I know you weren't drunk."

Sgt Mongkut stretched back in his chair and just stayed quiet. He knew the lieutenant was rightly focused on what steps to take next rather than on any dirty details about the scandal. Though the old man's own career was spotless, he was no stranger to managing others' nasty secrets. While he was also genuinely concerned about any personal stain upon his younger friend's well-earned reputation, more importantly he had to make certain the sergeant didn't make things worse.

"If that's how you're playing it! But I'm ordering you not to say a word. And you will confine yourself at home when not on duty. What are you smiling about now?"

"My apologies, sir, but am I allowed to at least step out to buy a paper?" Mongkut saw the lieutenant draw an inward grin from his impertinence. In the depths of his heart, the lieutenant knew this was in truth the worst of Mongkut's crimes.

"Well, suppose you do—not a word. And not in Petch-buri! Remember, not a word."

The sergeant pretended to zip his smile shut, rose and bowed, then quietly exited the office and maneuvered back to his desk. The fact that none of the other officers made a single crack about his eye made it perfectly clear they'd been trying to eavesdrop the entire time. Almost every unfounded fabrication known to man had been circulating around the department. The prevailing theme involved Mongkut having gotten blind drunk and starting a fistfight with a coconut vendor, neither of which was probable. Not a word, Mongkut kept reciting to himself, not a word.

Chapter 40: Where Things Had Come July 3rd 1997

Far overseas the annual burning of crops was starting to get out of control. Small rivulets of smoke converged high above Sumatra and Borneo into a brownish swath that blotted the garish tropical clouds as it began its slow slither northeast toward the unwitting peninsula. Little did the distant bustling cities of Singapore, Kuala Lumpur and Bangkok yet dream how hot and wildly the Indonesian peatlands would blaze across the strait this season, or how monstrous the ashy plumes would grow that were encroaching from over the waters to choke them dry. The historic fires of '97 now seem like ancient history anymore, along with all the other ill-fortune that bleak year finally brought.

*

Overhead, the sun was magnified in the mounting haze like a cruelly searing yolk. Mr Torpong scurried all up and down the streets distractedly, completely blind to the incredibly real threats that were rushing behind the scenes to cut down all his happiness. For so engrossed in his own internal thoughts had he become, Torpong never considered that he might still possess some smallest pieces. How could he? The rest of the world was swimming so madly before his hermit mind, he could hardly discern the very cracks in the sidewalk just beneath his aimless pilgrim feet.

...the art of the fugue is the act of falling forever. Rhythm and key expanding in unison unto the point where the whole of its cycle unfolds within the constraints of one encompassing measure. An entire civilization could subside between those two nodes...the beginning and the end. The drone of the wind between the tops of the skyscrapers, the emotive swells of the street traffic, the swarm of shoes that shuffle through their empty recitative. That jackhammer tearing itself into the corner there, its arrogant tat-tat-tat whose echo rolls and reverberates between opposing facades like a wave slowed with each rebound. Yes, a fugue perhaps. Giving shape to time, like music. Do not be baffled by the vocal arrangement, not by its ornamentation. It is always the one song alone and the same. Only in its counterpoint does it gain meaning...the composer signing his name in constant variation across an expanding universe. Until cut short of breath mid-measure...

Tolstoy's Rostov heard that fugue that dream-torn night before he was shot dead from his horse, facedown in the mud discoloring with his blood. I can feel its subterranean pulse, louder and louder. A veritable tide of sludge must at this very moment flow beneath my feet. Bangkok is afloat upon a sea of mud just waiting to suffocate

*its banks and up the sides of its walls. Coming to choke us out!
Oh how the population struggles in a graceful panic to rise above for
one more gasp. The cars and motorbikes racing in all contrariety,
pursuing who knows what...in truth they're only fleeing. The high-
rise offices, hotels and penthouses, forever reaching higher into the
sky...they too shall sink. And those nimble boatmen there—what
idiots they are if they think they might survive. Soon enough the
muck will eat away the boards and rust the bolts. They may as well
be sailing paper boats.*

*What were the words I saw this morning, ablaze across all the
papers?—'Baht plummets!'*... 'A broken lock, the rate of baht
and hint of rot'...*of course that's where their darkest fears must
lie. Take but a look into any pair of eyes. Fools every last one—
unto the end of time! I am falling. Saengdao is falling. You too,
Lek, you too are still falling, like a fruit from the tree. Bangkok
itself, I say, the whole of our city has been forever falling from its
first leap into futile flight. Falling to the tune of its own strange,
frightened chirping. Keep on! Keep on! I must keep on...!*

Torpong reached to touch the amulet beneath his shirt,
never stopping. How could the passing strangers guess at
the rushing impressions and ideas beneath the surface of
that solemn face? Even if one could listen in, the inward
monolog simply flowed on and on with no culminating
meaning, with no retraceable origin. Or perhaps instead
the thoughts of the lost and lonesome wanderer travel

like the shed leaf blown about the streets in circles until it's finally crunched beneath some unknown foot.

*

Saengdao was far from her husband at this moment and had neither the luxury nor heart to care where he'd managed to lose himself this time. She didn't even hear him leave the house. Her own particular sort of pit was opening up to swallow her down.

She'd been locked in her office since last night answering an increasingly uncontrollable series of telephone calls. It started with the one from the CEO, who would keep calling back with ever angrier but more useless orders. Saengdao was used to him hampering her work, but now, considering how dire the situation, her boss's interruptions seemed borderline sadistic. She kept her replies short, instinctively realizing that, as soon as she could get him off the phone, her top priority was to liquidate as many assets as possible. It was terrifying how quickly resources were freezing up, and it was impossible to find a foreign haven for what little she'd managed to pry free. Not a sane soul in the world wanted to own the crumbling baht anymore. For every call she made pleading for early payment, she received at least two from flustered creditors in return. Why had they borrowed so much in dollars? An already burdensome debt loomed ever higher with each small tick down of the THB. Her glance kept returning to that convulsing, failing line. The Nikkei would open soon with a whole new onslaught. Her boss would call again. It was like an invisible hand pulling a lose thread until the very fabric of the universe unraveled.

Saengdao's sisters and brothers kept calling too, each frantic with some unrelated, though strangely parallel plight. How could she concern herself with family now? They were like ghosts to her at the moment.

She'd warned the board about spreading themselves so thin. Why did the government refuse to step in and placate the horde of speculators? Letting the currency float was a death sentence to all of Thailand. Sleeplessness and disbelief were beginning to deaden her resolve. Her words grew hoarse and distracted; her aching eyes forgot that stupid line plummeting across her computer screen.

As Saengdao peered out her window onto the city below, listening apathetically to whoever's voice was on the other end, she believed she could already foresee what would follow next. Sure enough, subcontractors withdrew their bids. The next call was from the crew-chief demanding answers. Saengdao remembers how right at 4:03pm the last foreign financier pulled out. It all felt so predictable. Her powerlessness in truth began to bore her. Her thoughts turned inward where she clearly saw the final outcome. She was going to lose her job, lose the life she'd built. She'd have nothing left. Saengdao's unfinished tower was never going to reach completion.

And still the telephone rang and rang. And Saengdao decided she simply could no longer answer.

*

Saengdao died that night in a car crash. The police report would state she dozed off at the wheel. The authorities could not locate her husband until early the following morning. He was found asleep outdoors inside Lumpini Park. The night at last had brought some rest and small relief to the invalid...the stagnant night with its pathetic splotch of faintly shimmering stars.

"It's okay. You're not alone anymore," the officer said as he reached his hand into Torpong's sheltering shrub.

Chapter 41: Without End

Of all phenomena, perhaps the most perplexing is repetition.

As Yan leaned in perfect lonesomeness beneath a tree awaiting the start of school, he did not foresee the circle that was closing in on him. Anyone that read his stone-like face could see he'd withdrawn into a world impervious to ours. When Somchai approached, he found the boy's obliviousness a little disconcerting.

"Don't worry," he interrupted Yan's trance, "I'm not going to hurt you." He felt compelled to say it, though he could tell that Yan, who still wore the cut on his lip, was hardly worried at the moment. Yan remained silent.

"I've got this for you. There's more where that came from," Somchai said as he handed over the small sheet of paper he'd been holding. The corners of Yan's mouth tensed once he'd recognized it, for it belonged to him. It was his creation, though horribly stained and wrinkled.

On this particular page the Great Detective Yan and Doctor Toi were depicted reclining back in their office, smoking pipes (the lad's a bubble pipe) and reflecting upon how they'd managed to foil the sinister DMA once again. Yan had forgotten how stupid these comics could be—how divinely stupid. He might have smiled had it not been for Somchai's presence. Yan wasn't sure what to say.

"I know that it's yours. I know about—"

"About *what*?" Yan cut him off abruptly.

"Let's just say a certain ghost. Why don't we both just go and see? We should get out of here before the bell rings and somebody notices."

Yan glanced in the direction of the gates then back at Somchai. So, Fah had told someone else about Toi, though he'd asked her that night not to. Still, he could no longer consider it any great act of betrayal. He'd completely stopped thinking of Fah in such terms. Indeed until it'd plopped out right here from the horse's mouth that she'd divulged his secret, Yan believed he'd finally come to view her strictly objectively, with an almost mathematical degree of scrutiny.

But did she really believe him then? And might Somchai, who seemed to have been conjured out of air not so long ago, could he eventually come to believe in Toi too? The potential synthesis of these two metaphysically opposed impossibilities leant him a sort of absurd hope. He crumpled the page up into even worse shape than he'd received it and dropped it to the ground.

"Screw Nagani!" he ventured. "Right?"

No matter what trouble your reason continually warns you'll end up in, your gut emotion's going to drag your sorry and belabored body there through every mucky, reeking inch.

Sgt Mongkut was well aware not only of the professional risk, but also of the personal shame he'd endure if he was caught accosting the boy, though neither one sufficed to halt his trespass straight into the heart of Petchburi. The only thing that finally slowed his eager step was the timely ringing of the school bell from just around the corner. Never had that bell signaled showing up too late so sorrowfully.

*

That sound toned nothing sad for Pink. She listened to the fading bell with relish as she slid out from a wonderfully convenient corner. Now nothing stood in the way and she felt she ought to sprint the whole way there.

*

Yan followed Somchai as quietly as if he'd walked there by himself. His guide kept stopping along the way to buy and eat some sweets or to smoke another cigarette. Yan found it slightly amusing, though he stayed back the whole time like an obedient shadow. His mind began to wander to school, to what the other students must be studying. Lunchtime would be coming soon…

And while Yan had guessed it from the start, he hardly thought about the place he knew where they were going.

*

The sergeant recognized the truant flash of pink right away. It was a shot in the dark, but it was the best lead he had at the moment. Lucky for him it was a color of hair that stands out in a crowd, because the girl was cutting through the streets at a determined rate. When he followed her up and over the canal, Mongkut half-feared he'd run into the girl that'd smacked him with a coconut. He tried to pace himself, but that glimmer of pink just kept steadily receding in the distance. She appeared to be tracing the very path the boy once had, an assumption which the sergeant was soon forced to rely upon to guide his course. He had to admit he'd lost all sight of her once he reached Lumpini Park. He stopped inside to catch his breath.

It's hard to say when he first noticed the black wisp in the sky just beyond the trees, so subtle was it in registering upon his distracted consciousness. But once he'd fixed it in his mind, he kept looking up in its direction, then down again into the passing strangers' eyes to try and read a similarly stimulated sense of panic. Nothing—no

other soul appeared to see or care. The smoke rippled and
rose into the flawless blue from a broken building in the
distance, like from a half-burned incense stick.

*

When he reached the fence collapsing at the base of the
abandoned structure, a stray dog emerged and growled,
but showed no further appetite for confrontation. Mongkut could still make out the tiny billow of smoke issuing
from one of the paneless windows midway up. He pulled
out a pocket light and went about discovering the safest
way in.

One might well marvel over what obstacles cannot
prevent our reaching certain destinations. The sergeant
navigated the dark inside as much by pure imagination as
by his tiny light and the echo of his own small stumbles
and steps. Taking careful note of his progression up every
broken stair, over every pile of rubble, all he had to do
was envision his position inside the building versus where
he planned to go, and soon enough he was precisely there.

*

A wave of flashing smoke enveloped him when he burst
open the door. The combined smell of soot, feces and
urine was overwhelming. An unchecked conflagration
pulsed brightly inside, behind which hunched a ragged

shape. The figure crouching there was surrounded by heaps of crumpled waste that it mechanically fed into the flames while rocking back and forth and grunting. Mongkut approached to better make out the man.

"Are you okay? I'm here to help."

The squalid being did not answer but continued to groan and burn. There was something black dripping off the igniting papers.

"It's okay, you're not—"

Smoke choked Mongkut's breath and a shadow crossed his heart as he inched forward. He thought he might vomit from the stench when he knelt close to look into the stranger's grimy face. What could he do to stop his ranting? Why wouldn't the man acknowledge Mongkut's existence? A dangerous storm of embers whirled around the two like a million scorching feathers.

Mongkut reached his hand across the rhythmic tongues of flame to wipe away the ash from the one cracked eyeglass. And when he gazed into that man's one visible eye, the sergeant realized there was nothing left that he could do. He did not need to see into that other eye. It was the one face in the world he was in the worst position now to recognize. For that face was Mongkut's face...his own sad worn and troubled face. Though his was not the name which that face bore.

Nearing the end of their climb, Yan stopped in the middle of a stairway and let Somchai get ahead. A torn-away section in the wall had suddenly revealed to him an odd perspective.

In a remote sliver of light he saw two shapes leaning upon and caressing one another. The shifting tangle of sunlit pink and pigtails was unmistakable, their secret meaning as stark yet unattainable as any song's, a music that sang nothing beyond itself. Yan would've been content to gaze upon the two for an eternity.

But then a terrifying clang above broke their perfect silence.

Metal upon metal, again and again and again.

Yan knew he had no choice but to ascend into the blind resounding dark. He was too afraid to call back but hoped the girls had had the sense to run for their lives. A palpable black now rolled past in sickening rivulets. "There's fire!" he heard Somchai shout between the desperate peals.

A wild light thrashed in the outlined shadows just ahead. The chamber's door was smashed ajar—the very walls inside ablaze! And then—the arching silhouette of Somchai's arms and back reemerging out that fatal glow, dragging by its feet some heavy stubborn thing. "Help with him, damn it!" Somchai coughed and spit over the charred and smoldering corpse whose sacred name none but itself could speak thereafter.

Scott B Robinson writes and plays chess in Asheville, North Carolina. Learn more at fireandart.net.

Made in the USA
Columbia, SC
01 November 2023

24989606R00117